AF268782

Mistletoe & Motorcycles

MELANIE DAVIES

For everyone who just can't wait to deck the halls, light the tree, and fill their homes with Christmas cheer—yes, even in November ;)
May your holidays be as bright as your twinkling lights!

Author Note

Trigger Warnings:
Please be aware of potential triggers in this book.

THIS STORY CONTAINS:
- **Drug addiction** (not involving the main characters)
- **Sexual content**
- Brief mentions of **Alzheimer's/Dementia**

ADDITIONALLY, please note that this book is written in **British UK English**, following the Oxford style for spelling and grammar.

"You know, fate can't do everything on her own.
Sometimes, you have to make the first move."

MISTLETOE
And
Motorcycles

Chapter One

The bell above the door chimed, and I glanced up from the shelf I was rearranging. It was Wednesday, which could only mean one thing; he was here.

Ducking my head behind a row of paperbacks I was pricing up, I peered over the edge as he strolled in. Every Wednesday like clockwork. *He* would appear—tall, dark-haired, and wrapped in a worn leather jacket that made him look more like he belonged in a moody black-and-white movie than in Jamestown's only bookstore.

There was something about him, this quiet stranger who drifted in and out of my week, that kept my gaze lingering far too long.

He glanced around briefly before heading to the same set of shelves he always did. For weeks now, I'd watched him walk in, browse, choose one book, and leave.

Today, I had strategically positioned myself to be in his line of sight. I'd spent nearly ten minutes rearranging a stack of romance novels just to be within earshot when he showed up.

Every week, I promised myself that *this* time I'd say

something, anything, to start a conversation. Maybe ask him about his favourite book. Or why he only came in on Wednesdays, maybe he lived close by?

Today, though, felt different. Maybe it was the confidence boost from my favourite green sweater or the simple fact that I was tired of watching him from afar. I had to say something—*anything*. After all, I'd grown up here, and I'd never had trouble chatting with the regulars. But he was different, with his dark, intense gaze that always seemed a thousand miles away. He'd probably find me boring and provincial, the small-town bookshop girl with dorky looking glasses.

He reached out for a book and I tensed, feeling my palms go clammy against the paperbacks I was holding. I took a slow breath, hoping it would steady me enough to blurt out something casual and clever.

"So...what brings you to Jamestown?" I imagined myself asking, with an easy-going smile. But as I tried to form the words, they felt clumsy and awkward on my tongue, like a language I barely knew.

"Holly!" Mrs. Finch called from the counter, snapping me back to the present. Startled, I straightened up and tried to look busy. My cheeks burned as I realised I'd been staring at him. Again.

"Have you restocked the new arrivals display yet?"

"I'm on it," I managed, grateful for the excuse to step away. But I snuck one more glance over my shoulder before heading to the storage room. He was still flipping through the pages, his eyes scanning over the words with that same focused, far-off look he always had. I couldn't help but wonder what he thought about, what went on behind those eyes that made him so different from everyone else around here.

In the cramped storage room, I gathered up a stack of

new releases, though my mind was still out front with the stranger. I knew his name was Dylan—he'd mentioned it once to Mrs. Finch. He usually selected books from the sci-fi, horror or dystopian section. He seemed so out of place here, like he'd just wandered into our sleepy little town by mistake and had somehow gotten stuck. Or maybe he was on his way to some big adventure, the kind I'd always dreamed of having.

When I came back out, Dylan had drifted to the horror section, a book in hand. For a split second I thought he was heading to the counter, but instead, he put the book back on the shelf and moved toward the door. My heart sank—he was leaving. Again, and this time he didn't buy a new book.

I kept my eyes low, trying not to stare, but I couldn't help glancing up as he reached the door. And just like that, our eyes met. For one heart-pounding moment, he looked at me, an unreadable expression flickering across his face. Then he nodded, just barely, and turned to leave.

The bell chimed again and I exhaled slowly, clutching the pile of new releases to my chest as I watched him walk out. Maybe next time I'd actually say something instead of hiding. It wasn't that I was shy, exactly; I just didn't know how to talk to someone like him, someone who seemed like one of those popular guys from high school. The ones with the blondes draped in his arms. A player.

Mrs. Finch's voice broke into my thoughts. "Holly, when you've done that, I need you to fix up the window display. It's not Christmas enough."

"Sure thing Mrs Finch," I murmured, still staring at the door he'd disappeared through.

The faint sound of a motorcycle engine roared from outside as another customer came in. I caught a glimpse of Dylan putting on a helmet before he sped off down the street. Of course, he drove a motorcycle.

"You know, fate can't do everything on her own," she said, watching my eyes dart back to her. Did she know I'd been staring at him this entire time? "Sometimes, you have to make the first move."

I bit my lip, my thoughts drifting to the tall stranger with the dark eyes who came in every week. Maybe Mrs. Finch was right. Perhaps it was time to stop dreaming about adventures and start living them, one small step at a time. Maybe next Wednesday, I'd finally find the courage to say hello.

Once I'd used the last can of fake snow spray on the windows, the early evening had already settled in. Mrs. Finch cashed up the till for the day while I locked the front door and turned the key to bring the window shutters down.

There was always a sense of calm during the evenings when the sunset, and a light mist of rain covered the ground. After sending me on my way, Mrs. Finch waved goodbye and I bundled myself up in my woolly hat and coat. I caught the same bus I always did and headed home.

The following Wednesday, my mystery man didn't come into the store, and I was left feeling a little disappointed.

Chapter Two

Three weeks passed, and I was beginning to think he was just a passerby. We often got them in this small town—people visiting elderly grandparents, tourists interested in the historical sites, or those just looking for a quiet break.

Mrs. Finch was off today, leaving just Kieren and me to manage the shop. Kieren, Mrs. Finch's son, would eventually inherit this old bookstore when she retired—a fact he constantly reminded me of. I'd been here for the past four years, and although I'd progressed to "shop organiser" and "ordering girl," as they both called me, I felt stuck in a loop.

It was always the same routine; open the store, greet customers, recommend books, organise the old ladies' book club. Occasionally, we'd host a semi-famous author for a book signing, but that was as exciting as it got.

Jamestown wasn't a place you came for adventure. It was a place you came to grow old.

I leaned against the counter, watching the clock on the computer. I'd seen every hour so far, and there was only so much cleaning I could do without Kieren pointing out that I was "doing nothing."

"Mom needs you to do the inventory on the comics, by the way! If you're not too busy, that is."

Kieren's voice called from the office behind me where he sat with his feet propped up on the desk, leaning back in his chair with his baseball cap pulled low over his clearly closed eyes.

He was such a pompous, lazy, annoying man. I hated working with him. Considering he was Mrs. Finch's son—who was always pleasant and warm with customers—Kieren was nothing like her. Quick to temper, he rarely wanted to do anything involving actual labour and only seemed interested in how much money the store made each day.

With a sigh, I pulled out the inventory folder from under the counter, grabbed a pen, and headed toward the back of the store. If the bell rang, Kieren would just have to get up and work the till while I was back here, hiding.

Mumbling to myself, I popped in one earbud to listen to my audiobook, *A Christmas Wish* by Lyndsey Day, this month's book club selection for the old ladies. I always tried to read or listen to their choices so I could discuss them together. Even if nine times out of ten it was an over-the-top romance where the women were either desperate for a man or helpless damsels, this one was interesting enough.

I pulled out stacks of comics, checking each one against the names on the list and noting any new arrivals. Mrs. Finch wasn't the best at tracking what came in, and sometimes she'd misplace a customer's order or number, leaving them frustrated when we hadn't contacted them.

Since I'd taken over the inventory, these incidents had been minimised. Organisation was something I loved; it kept my busy mind quiet.

When two black boots appeared beside me, I didn't pay much attention to them, assuming it was just another customer. I was deep in my notes, with the sounds of the main characters in my audiobook professing their love after only fifteen chapters. Then, a comic book fell from the shelf above and landed on my head, snapping me out of my trance.

Ready to scold a clumsy teenager, I turned, only to feel my breath hitch as I found myself face-to-face with my mystery man. He bent down to pick up the comic, an apology already on his lips.

"Sorry about that, I was trying to reach a different one."

Words failed me. I could barely utter a sound as I stammered and tried to hide the sudden blush creeping up my cheeks. *Idiot, now's your chance!* my inner voice screamed, urging me to say something, anything, instead of just staring at him. He even smelled good up close. And his eyes—they weren't as dark as I'd thought. They had hints of green and brown.

"That's... that's alright. Is there anything I can help with?" I finally managed, pulling out my earbud and shoving it into my pocket, giving him my full attention.

He smirked—a half-smile, really, and I could have sworn I saw a hint of a dimple.

"Nah, that's okay. I'm good."

His voice was like something out of a romance movie, deep and husky, with a hint of mischief at the end of his sentence. He was more than I'd imagined, standing right there in front of me.

I nodded, unsure where to go from here. I couldn't just continue a conversation with a complete stranger who didn't want my help. Sighing a little, I went back to my notes, trying to ignore the butterflies in my stomach and the fact that I could still feel his eyes on me. Soon enough, though, he went about his business and left the comic book section, heading toward the horror stacks, and I breathed a sigh of relief.

By the time I'd finished inventorying the final comic, I half expected him to have gone, but instead, I found him sitting in one of the customer chairs, flipping through a horror graphic novel.

I'd nearly forgotten about that little reading corner. The only people who usually used it were teenagers sneaking in to read the latest smutty fantasy novels, hoping their parents wouldn't find out. The book club, on the other hand, preferred the other side of the store, where a table with chairs had been set up at their request.

"There you are!" shouted Kieren from the other side of the stacks. "There are customers here waiting to be served."

"Well, serve them, Kieren. I'm busy doing this," I replied, holding up the folder as if I had more work to do. He scoffed, shooting me a nasty look before stomping off toward the front of the store.

"Asshole," I muttered, clutching the folder tightly to my chest.

"He is a bit, isn't he?"

"Bloody hell!" I yelped, the folder slipping from my hands as I nearly jumped out of my skin.

Dylan stood there, chuckling to himself as he bent down to pick up my folder and notes. I hadn't even noticed he'd left his chair and was standing next to me. I really wasn't paying much attention today.

"Sorry, you shouldn't have heard that," I managed to say once my heart stopped pounding.

"I didn't mean to frighten you." He handed me my things. "Is that guy your boss?"

"He wishes. He's my boss's son, supposedly working here to get used to the store. He's about as useful as a chocolate teapot."

Dylan stifled a laugh, holding his graphic novel in one hand, and we both noticed the pen I'd dropped at the same time. As we bent down together, our fingers brushed, and the butterflies from earlier began to dance under my skin again. He let me grab the pen and took a step back, creating space between us—which, honestly, was a relief. It gave me room to breathe again.

"Was there anything I could help you with?" I offered again, clearing my throat to break the silence that now loomed between us.

"Actually, I was wondering if you had book two of this series?"

He held up the graphic novel he'd been reading. I didn't recognise the title—it wasn't a genre I read—but a quick search through our system could fix that. Thankfully, there was a small computer tucked down one of the stacks that would do just the job.

"I can check the system for you," I said, giving my best customer service smile as I led him toward the autobiography aisle. It was always quiet down here; barely anyone ventured this way unless they were a university student doing research. Most of our regulars were either elderly folk or young teens.

"What was the author's name again?"

Setting down my folder beside me, I pulled out the keyboard drawer and powered up the computer. Dylan showed me the book.

"G.J. Lewis," he replied. Typing his name into the system, a long list of books by the same author scrolled down the screen. He must have written over a hundred novels, and it took me a few minutes to scan through and see what we had in-store and what we could order. But, unfortunately, no book two was listed.

"We can order it for you, if you'd like? It'll take a few days, though," I offered.

"Yeah, sure, that'd be great! I can swing by next Wednesday if that's alright? Do I pay now or later?"

"You can pay on collection. Let me just pop this through for you. I will, however..." I hesitated, unsure how to word the next part without sounding creepy. "I will need your number—to contact you when it arrives."

Dylan smiled as he took out his phone and handed it to me, opening up the number keypad.

"Or, I can take yours if that's easier?"

"Mine?" I stammered, glancing between his phone and his face, confused. "You'd only need the store's number."

"How will I get in touch with you if I want to take you out for coffee before then?"

I was stunned by how smooth he was. I hadn't expected that; I'd convinced myself he was just a book-loving guy. I'd imagined plenty of scenes in my head, but none of them went quite like this. My mind froze, the words stuck somewhere in my throat.

"If that's alright with you?" His grin had that same sly charm.

"Umm, sure. That's fine with me."

I managed to blurt out, keying in my number and handing him back the phone, which he promptly used to call me, making my phone buzz in my pocket.

"My name's Dylan, by the way." He extended his hand, and I took it nervously.

"Holly. My parents love Christmas," I added, cringing internally at my awkwardness.

We smiled at each other as we shook hands, and soon I was following Dylan back to the front of the store, processing his order for both books before he headed out the door. As it clicked shut, *wow*, I finally let out a breath, feeling my heart begin to slow.

Chapter Three

By the time the weekend arrived, my first break in nearly three months, I sat at my small dining table in my very small one-bedroom studio apartment. My cat, Usagi—named after Sailor Moon—meowed insistently at my ankles. Even though I'd already fed her this morning, she acted as if I was starving her.

Sipping my warm tea and taking a bite of my very buttery toast, I tried to decide what to do with my day. My parents were away on their usual Christmas holiday in Austria, and wouldn't be back for another week. As much as I would have loved to join them, I'd chosen to stay home.

Silly me.

My only friend, Becky, was busy with her boyfriend, visiting his parents in the city. And while there were small Christmas markets opening this weekend as well as the town lights being turned on, I wasn't sure I could face the endless questions I'd get from everyone asking why I was still here instead of moving away after university.

My English Literature honours degree hung above my bed in a glittery silver frame Becky gifted me, next to a photo of me holding my diploma with my parents. I'd come back here after university, and now I felt stuck.

"You know, fate can't do everything on her own. Sometimes, you have to make the first move."

Mrs. Finch's words echoed in my mind, reminding me that the only reason I felt stuck was because I wasn't making any moves myself. Which was silly, really—I was the creator of my fate, and only I could change things.

Feeling a spark of confidence, I pulled up my phone contacts and saw Dylan's number, the last call I'd received that wasn't from my mom. I hadn't yet added him to my contacts, especially since he hadn't messaged me.

Swallowing my nerves, I tapped the message icon and began typing something. Then deleted it. Retyped. Deleted again—until finally, I settled on something that didn't sound too ridiculous.

I was a twenty-three-year-old woman with barely any relationship experience beyond a few university boyfriends, and Dylan seemed nice enough.

> Hi Dylan, it's Holly. The girl from the bookstore. I was wondering if you wanted to go watch the Christmas lights get turned on this evening? No probs if not, of course! Let me know 😊

Pressing send, I flipped my phone face down on the table. My leg bounced nervously as I waited, no longer able to eat my breakfast. I hated sending texts, especially risky ones like this. I'd never made the first move before; I was an introvert. A happy one, at that.

Then the phone vibrated. Holding my breath, I flipped it over and saw the notification from his number. *He replied!* It's probably a polite no, I thought as I opened it, biting my lip.

He didn't like Christmas? That made me a little sad, considering my apartment was already decked out with Christmas decorations, fairy lights, and a colourful tree. But at least he was saying yes to doing *something*.

I stared at the screen for a few seconds, letting it sink in. He'd actually said yes. Glancing up, I caught sight of myself in the mirror. Bedhead from last night, yesterday's eyeliner smudged under my eyes, and I was pretty sure there was peanut butter smeared on my t-shirt. Looking at my reflection with wide eyes, I knew I couldn't leave the apartment looking like this.

Quickly texting him back, I typed:

Satisfied, I set my phone down and headed to the bathroom for a shower and to tame the beehive that was my brown hair.

ONCE WASHED, dried, and dressed in the cutest maroon sweater dress I owned paired with thick black tights and brown ankle boots, I took one look at myself in my wardrobe mirror and sighed. *This is the best it's going to get.* I wasn't the type of girl to dress up. I was more of a leggings-

and-comfy-t-shirt kind of person, or I was in my work uniform.

No, you can't wear this—it's just coffee. Second-guessing myself, I checked the time on my phone. I still had another hour until I needed to leave, plenty of time to change. I threw on a pair of jeans that were a little too tight, a plain dark orange t-shirt, my fleece-lined jacket, and my Vans. *That's better.* I felt more like myself.

"It's just coffee, Holly. Get a grip!" I muttered. Usagi meowed at me from her cat tree as I sat down on the edge of my bed.

The teenager inside me was a bundle of nerves. I wasn't the kind of person who went out of her way to meet people for coffee or even to make new friends. Heck, I really only had one close friend, since most of my university friends now lived all over the world.

Rather than sitting here, I decided I could walk into town. The bus would be faster, but walking might help clear my mind and relax me. Thankfully, the forecast was clear and cold, so a hat would be needed.

Wrapping my scarf around my neck and tucking it into my jacket, I popped on my hat and grabbed my small back-pack. I wasn't a handbag person; backpacks were better since I could fit my Kindle or at least a book inside.

After topping up Usagi's food bowl, I gave her a little kiss on the head and said my goodbyes. With one earbud in, I headed out the door, down the stairwell, and onto the street outside my apartment block. I'd rather be early than late.

Chapter Four

I wrapped my scarf a little tighter, tucking my chin into the soft wool as I walked toward the town centre. Rounding the corner, I couldn't help the grin that spread across my face. Jamestown had fully embraced Christmas, and everywhere I looked, there were signs of the season. Shop doorways were decked with evergreen garlands and twinkling fairy lights, and almost every window had a wreath with a bright red bow. Even the lampposts were wrapped in ribbons and strings of lights, glowing warmly in the cold evening air.

Christmas in town had always been my favourite time of year. There was a cosy magic that settled over everything—a mix of nostalgia and cheer that made the town feel brighter and more alive. But knowing that Dylan wasn't a fan of Christmas had taken a little of the glow from it. I didn't quite understand, but maybe I could help him see it in a new way, maybe lift his spirits a bit. I'd been lucky enough to grow up with all of this, with all the warmth of Jamestown at Christmas time.

I was a bit early to meet him, so I strolled through the crowd, taking my time and browsing the Christmas market stalls that had popped up all along the square. The town was buzzing with people—it was the busiest I'd ever seen it. From a small stage in the centre of the square, a local choir was singing a familiar carol, the soft harmonies drifting over the square. Just behind them stood the town's Christmas tree, tall and grand, dressed in red, silver and gold ornaments, waiting for its lights to be switched on.

The stalls were packed with holiday goodies, and I couldn't resist stopping at one filled with handmade ornaments. I picked up a small wooden snowflake, its edges carefully burned to show delicate patterns. It was lovely and would be a perfect addition to my tree at home. I smiled, already feeling a little extra Christmas magic just holding it.

A few stalls over, I found wood-burned decor with warm messages like *"Joy to the World"* and *"Peace on Earth."* I ran my fingers over a beautiful plaque that said, *"Home for the Holidays"* and imagined it on my wall, filling my apartment with that extra bit of holiday cheer.

The smells around me were heavenly—there was a stall selling steaming cups of mulled wine, the scent of warm spices filling the air. Across from it was the sweet aroma of roasting marshmallows. I couldn't resist grabbing a skewer and roasting one myself over the open flame. The marshmallow turned perfectly golden, soft and gooey, and I took a bite, the warmth and sweetness reminding me of winter nights with my parents, gathered around the fire.

I checked my watch—still a bit early for my meeting with Dylan. I closed my eyes for a second, breathing in the crisp, spiced air and letting myself soak in the joy around me. This was what Christmas felt like, what made it so special to me.

Maybe, just maybe, I could help Dylan see it too. If I could find a way to share just a bit of the holiday magic, maybe he'd feel it. With that thought in mind, I decided to get him a cup of mulled wine as a little taste of Christmas spirit. Maybe it would be enough to make tonight a little warmer for him too.

By the time I was supposed to meet him, I stood near the entrance of the bookstore, which had closed early to prepare for the lights event. When Dylan appeared, he was dressed in nearly all black except for a dark red scarf. I couldn't help but admire him, holding the cup close to my chest, its warmth radiating through my hands.

"Hi! I hope you don't mind—I got you some mulled wine," I said with a smile, offering him the cup as he approached.

"Thanks, but I'm not a fan of the stuff." He shook his head, popping his hands into his pockets.

"Oh, never mind, then—more for me!" I smiled, hoping to cover my embarrassment. "Shall we head to the café?"

He nodded, and we began the short walk to the café I often escaped to for lunch. As we passed by, I noticed Frank, the homeless man I usually saw in the mornings, tucked away in a doorway. I held the mulled wine out to him instead.

"I'll bring you breakfast tomorrow, Frank, don't worry," I said kindly.

He gave me a bright smile, hugging the cup close to his chest. With the evenings getting colder, I really hoped he'd find somewhere warm soon.

I could feel Dylan's eyes on me, watching closely as we reached the café door. He opened it for me, gesturing for me to enter first, and we found a small two-person booth near the window.

The whole place was decorated with fairy lights, Christmas garlands, and each table had a red tablecloth draped over it. Christmas songs played quietly in the background, and I noticed Dylan sigh as he glanced around before sitting across from me.

"If you don't like it, we can go somewhere else?" I offered.

"No, it's fine. This town just likes Christmas a little too much for any normal person's liking."

Taken aback by the roughness in his voice, I lowered my eyes to the menu in front of me. *This is turning out to be a great evening,* I thought sarcastically. Maybe we should've picked somewhere else, somewhere quieter—and definitely less festive.

"Sorry," he said softly. "I just have a few bad memories tied to Christmas."

"That's alright. Sometimes it can be a bit much—I get it. I mean, I'm literally named after the festive *Holly,* so I get it."

He chuckled a little under his breath just as the waitress arrived. She was dressed like a reindeer, her apron adorned with a deer design, and antlers perched on top of her head. Her smile was as dazzling as those in a Christmas movie.

"What can I get you two?" she asked, chewing a piece of gum. She wasn't the regular server I'd met here before, but they probably hired more staff for the holiday rush.

"I'll have a vanilla latte, please, with oat milk," I said.

"I'll have a black coffee, please, and oat milk in one of those little pourer things," Dylan added.

Once the waitress left, a slightly uncomfortable silence fell between us as Dylan stared out the window at the square, bustling with Christmas festivities. Luckily, the waitress returned quickly, setting down our drinks with a couple of complimentary shortbread biscuits.

"Are you from here, Dylan?" I asked, trying to break the ice.

"My grandmother is—she moved back here when I went to college." He stirred his coffee, adding three heaping spoonful's of sugar, and I listened intently. "I'm originally from Seoul."

I almost spat out my sip of coffee. Seoul? Out of all the places in the world, he wound up here. That got me hooked. I needed to know everything.

"And you wound up here? — That's pretty sad actually, out of everywhere in the world Jamestown is not a place you just find either. You're grandmothers from here? Is your mom too?"

Sipping on his cup of coffee, he seemed to be lost in thought for a moment. Perhaps unsure of how to answer my questions, maybe he didn't want to for as far as we were concerned, we were still strangers to one another.

"My mom met my dad on some kinda girls holiday. He's from South Korea, and they stayed together for a while. But my paternal grandparents weren't too impressed with the whole idea so when I was about six, she left my dad and moved back here," he paused, taking another drink and fidgeting with a silver ring on his thumb.

"I moved to Korea when I was about sixteen, and the only reason I've come back is mom has disappeared, off with her new boyfriend and left my grandmother to fend for herself."

His shoulders slumped a little as he spoke of the sudden responsibility he was given. A whole life ahead of him and having to be stuck here. I was a little envious, he'd obviously seen some of the world and possibly more.

"Sounds like your life got turned upside down a bit." I commented. He mmm'ed and continued to drink his coffee.

"You're from here I take it?" He asked, his brown eyes staring at me.

I gave a small nod in return, I was born and bred in Jamestown. I secretly hated it here, but never had the courage to leave, not fully anyway.

"My parents met in college, had me and well, that's about as exciting as it gets. I did leave for college, but I still came back." I admitted. Saying it out loud always made me realise how boring I must have seemed.

"Would you leave tomorrow if you could?" He asked, leaning back in his chair and popping an arm on the back of it. He seemed more relaxed than when we arrived.

"If the funds were there and I could take my cat, yes."

His eyes perked up a little at the mention of my cat, almost with excitement. For someone who dressed so stand-offish and had that cool demeanour about him, I couldn't help but find his change in expressions cute.

"I like cats." He said, with a small hint of a smile, "I had one growing up. His name was Jazz."

"That's a good name for a cat. You will need to meet Usagi one day."

His eyes widened even more then, leaning forward as his face lit up.

"You named your cat after Sailor Moon?"

I couldn't help but laugh at his excitement, no one ever got it when I mentioned Usagi's name or the fact I was a raging Sailor Moon fan. It was the only show I could get in college that kept me up through studying for exams. Well, that was until it became more of a distraction, and I was hooked into the whirlwind storyline of the moon kingdom and the sailor scouts.

"I sure did. She's the best character in the world, after all," I replied.

"Well, I wouldn't say *the* best. Goku could easily take her."

He leaned back in his chair, looking pretty smug, and I had to hold back from geeking out to prove him wrong.

"If Goku got in close, maybe he'd have a chance. But Usagi's powers—especially as Eternal Sailor Moon—she can literally destroy and recreate universes! She'd totally beat him." I crossed my arms, nodding confidently.

He laughed, a full chuckle, and I couldn't help but laugh a little back. Suddenly, the tension in the air seemed to disappear. I felt my shoulders relax as I took a sip of my coffee. The café was starting to fill up with people coming in from outside, some grabbing drinks to go, others settling in at tables.

Though Jamestown didn't have the hustle and bustle of a big city, there was rarely a dull day here.

Frank had wandered inside, and the waitress, all smiles, sat him down with a warm cup of coffee. A few minutes later, she returned with a slice of cake and a bowl of hot soup, her smile bright as starlight. Frank mirrored her warmth with his own smile, and for a moment, they seemed to be in their own little bubble.

"Have you always helped people in need?" Dylan asked suddenly. I hadn't realised I'd been staring at Frank and the waitress.

"Oh, yeah. I try whenever I can," I said, tucking a strand of hair behind my ear. "I volunteer at the homeless shelter a few times a month, or at least whenever I have the time. My parents always taught me to give back as much as possible." I paused, feeling a little nervous. "You said you're here to look after your grandmother. Is there anything I can do to help?"

He lifted a shoulder in a half shrug and ran a hand through his hair, sitting a little straighter as he finished his drink.

"Unless you can help her get mobile, I don't think there's much to be done. She refuses to leave the house at this point."

"Hmm... what about getting her to join the book club we host at the store?" I suggested. "I could bring her this month's book, or you could take it to her, and if she enjoys it, maybe you could bring her along next time. The meetings are on the last Saturday of the month."

He tilted his head, looking at me with those deep brown eyes and a half smile. Maybe he thought my suggestion was a good idea—or maybe he thought I was crazy for imagining his grandma would join a book club. He didn't say anything right away, just gestured to the waitress to top up his coffee while I was still only halfway through on my own.

Placing his hands on the table, Dylan wrapped his fingers around his mug as I watched his every movement, mesmerised by his hands, his presence, his very body. I'd never been so instantly drawn to someone. I'd read stories where the heroine falls for the main guy at first sight, and I'd always laughed at the idea—love at first sight wasn't real. And yet, the butterflies in the pit of my stomach weren't just nerves. There was definitely something there... maybe even a little lust and wonder.

"Do you drive, Holly?" he asked, breaking my thoughts.

I shook my head, shrugging. "Never really needed to."

"Ever been on the back of a motorcycle before?"

My eyes widened at the idea. A motorcycle? My parents would lose it if they found out I'd dared to try something so... dangerous. I crossed my ankles just to get my one bouncing leg to stop.

"No, I've never ridden one."

"Do you want to?"

Before I could respond, he stood up, holding out a hand, and a shiver ran down my spine as my fingers brushed his. He couldn't be serious, could he? Without waiting for me to answer, Dylan tossed a few bills onto the table to cover the check and tip, then gently pulled me from the booth.

"Come on."

He led me out of the café, past the bookstore, and

through a small crowd until we reached a narrow alleyway where his motorcycle was chained to a bike rack.

I didn't know much about motorcycles, but this one was sleek and black, with a few silver details that gleamed under the streetlight. Resting on the seat were two helmets, one plain black and the other marked with a silver lightning bolt. He lifted the plain one and held it out to me.

"Were you expecting me to say yes?" I teased.

"Hoping, yeah."

He flashed that same irresistible smile, the one that made my knees go weak. Suddenly, his hand was in my hair, lightly tugging the band holding up my ponytail, letting my hair fall loose. My heart skipped a beat at how close he was, his scent—a mix of fresh air and sweet aftershave—making it hard to keep my cool.

"You know how to put one of these on?" he asked, holding up the helmet.

He didn't return my hair tie, slipping it onto his wrist instead as he gently placed the helmet on my head, securing the strap beneath my chin. My breath caught, my gaze fixed on him. He made something as simple as putting on a helmet look unbelievably sexy.

"There. Now, hop on and hold on tight."

He didn't have to tell me twice.

Chapter Five

The engine rumbled beneath me and I tightened my arms around Dylan's waist, my heart thumping in sync with the motorcycle. This was nothing like a car ride. There were no doors to protect me, no seatbelt, nothing but my grip and Dylan's steadying presence keeping me secure.

We eased out onto the main street, and I felt the thrill rush through me as the bike gained speed. The town lights blurred around us, a mix of warm yellows and whites, but I barely noticed them. My senses were heightened, every breeze brushing against me like an electric jolt, the smell of asphalt and leather filling my lungs.

I held on tighter as we turned a corner, leaning instinctively with him, and the movement was so smooth it felt like dancing. I glanced to the side and saw people walking the sidewalks, heads turning as we passed. Part of me wished I could wave, but I gripped him tighter instead, laughing against the helmet as the road stretched out in front of us.

As we rode through town, the familiar buildings of Jamestown zipped past—the old library, the small supermarket, even Greenfield Pub looked different from this angle, almost like I was seeing the town for the first time. Soon, the streetlights started to fade as we made our way toward the open road.

The night air turned cooler, sharper, and I felt it sting my hands. Taking one hand off the handlebars, Dylan found my fingers and pushed one hand into his pocket, and I copied him on the other side. Maybe I should have worn gloves. Dylan picked up speed, and a part of me screamed that it was too fast, too reckless, but I bit my lip, determined not to show any fear. Instead, I focused on the sound of the engine, the rhythm of the wind against my jacket, and the thrill of freedom that stretched out with every passing mile.

Then, as the road curved, I saw it ahead—the cliff's edge, dark against the horizon. I'd heard about this place for years, the spot where teenagers went to make out, drink, and get away from their parents. But I'd never been here, not like this, and definitely not with someone like Dylan.

He slowed down as we approached, and the bike coasted to a stop. The silence settled around us as he turned off the engine. I took a breath, still clinging to him, realising that I hadn't let go since we started.

"You can let go now," he said, his voice teasing as he glanced back at me.

"Oh—right." I laughed, pulling my arms back and flexing my fingers, which were slightly numb. "I... Wow. I didn't expect it to be like that."

He grinned, pulling off his helmet and ruffling his hair. "It's something, isn't it?"

"Something," I echoed, hopping off the bike, my legs shaky. As they touched solid ground, he placed his hands on my shoulders so I could get the feeling back in my legs, and then unclipped the helmet.

"Glad you enjoyed it." He said, lifting the helmet off and placing it back on the bike.

I looked out over the cliff's edge, the town lights of Jamestown tiny and twinkling in the distance. The quiet wrapped around us, broken only by the soft hum of the highway far below.

Taking a deep breath as my adrenaline started to fade, I turned to face Dylan. He leaned against his bike with a knowing smile.

"You know what? I think I kind of loved it." I laughed, feeling a sudden joy blooming in my chest.

I understood now why so many people in movies owned bikes—the thrill of freedom was like nothing else. It felt almost as if I were flying, and I could see how addictive that feeling might get. I was already looking forward to the next ride, even if it was just to head home.

"I started coming up here when someone told me about the view," he muttered, crossing his arms as he looked out over the horizon.

"Oh, not for all the young ladies?" I teased, glancing back at the sparkling town below.

He chuckled and came to stand beside me, our shoulders almost touching. The butterflies were still there, but they didn't dance as nervously as before. Being close to him on the bike had settled my nerves, at least for the moment.

"You're honestly the only young lady I've come across up here."

I smiled, finding it easy to believe him. "That sounds about right. We're a rare breed, us youngsters."

Talking to Dylan felt so natural. At first, he'd made me feel like a silly schoolgirl with a make-believe crush whenever he came into the store. I'd pretend to be busy, clearing shelves, stocking books, or pottering around just to catch a glimpse of him. I'd wanted to talk to him so many times, but my shyness always held me back. The way he looked, the way he moved, even the way he spoke to Mrs. Finch—I couldn't help but wonder what kind of person he was.

He was honestly too handsome to be talking to me.

"You've always worn glasses?" he asked, breaking me from my thoughts.

"Yep, since I was a kid. Blessed with short-sightedness," I replied with a smirk.

"Have you ever thought of contacts?"

"Once, but the idea of sticking my finger in my eye freaked me out too much." I paused, side-eyeing him as he looked down at me. My eyes barely reached his shoulder— our heights were definitely mismatched. "Do the glasses bother you?" I asked suddenly.

He smiled, leaning a little closer. "Not at all. Not your fault you're pretty much blind."

I rolled my eyes, stifling a laugh, feeling completely at ease with him. It made me happy. Now, I just had to get him to start liking Christmas. And maybe, if he wanted to hang out again, I'd eventually learn why he didn't like it in the first place.

We spent a while just looking out over the horizon, until it began to get a little chilly. My jeans and jacket did little to keep the heat in, and I was grateful for Dylan's warmth as we rode back into town and stopped at the same café from earlier.

This time, instead of coffee, we had hot chocolate in takeaway cups and wandered through town, now lit up with Christmas lights. The crowds had died down a bit. It was still busy, but not so packed that you had to worry about crowd control.

A small-town fair had arrived early this morning, and nearly everyone was riding the Merry-Go-Round, Ferris Wheel, Bumper Cars, or the Waltzer's. How anyone could dislike this time of year, I would never understand. Dylan huffed a little as the scent of cinnamon filled the air, and I tried not to laugh at his discomfort. Cinnamon was definitely an acquired taste, and I had to agree—it could be a little much.

We sipped our hot chocolates, watching small children laugh on the rides with their parents, groups of teenage boys showing off for the girls, and even an elderly couple sneaking a quick peck on the Ferris Wheel.

This year, a small ice-skating rink had been set up for the public. People-watching was bound to be my favourite activity this year, as many first-time skaters clung to the sides, used little penguin guides, or fell repeatedly on their bums.

"You ever ice skate?" I asked Dylan as we sat on a bench across from the rink, watching the scene.

"It's pretty big in Seoul during the holidays," he said. "We usually get snow by late December. Christmas is more like a second Valentine's Day; couples and families go out together."

I found myself captivated by his voice, eager to learn more about his culture. I'd only read about Korea in history books or watched the odd K-drama, and the language always sounded beautiful.

"Can you speak Korean?" I asked.

"Fluently. My father and grandparents didn't allow English in the house, so I learned it young and had to relearn it when I went back."

Just then, the sound of someone else falling on the ice drew my attention. When I turned back, Dylan was tossing our empty cups into the bin.

"How do you say, 'thank you' in Korean?" I asked, curious.

"Gamsahabnida."

"Gamsenamda." I attempted, and Dylan chuckled, shaking his head.

"No, no, it's 'gam-sa-ham-ni-da.' Try again."

Blushing as I clearly butchered the word, I tried again. "Gam-saham-ni-da... Gamsahamnida."

"Much better," he smiled. "You'll be speaking fluent Korean in no time!"

I rolled my eyes, grinning as we turned back to watch the skaters. After a while, we joined the queue for hot dogs and strolled through the fair. Dylan noticed me shivering and insisted on draping his jacket over my shoulders. Though it was huge on me, he didn't seem bothered by the cold, even with just a hoodie on. He was definitely an Elsa, and I couldn't resist humming a bit of *Let It Go* under my breath.

⚜

SITTING on the back of his motorcycle, my arms wrapped around Dylan's waist, I tucked my hands into his pockets to keep warm. As he drove me back to my apartment, I couldn't help wishing I could invite him in, but with clothes scattered everywhere from my many outfit changes, I thought better of it.

"Thank you for an enjoyable evening," I said, handing him the spare helmet as he took his off.

He switched off the bike, placed both helmets on the seat, and gestured toward my front door.

"What kind of gentleman would I be if I didn't at least walk you to your doorstep?"

He was nothing like I'd imagined—the "bad boy player"

image I'd expected with the motorcycle was so far from reality. Instead, he was kind, easy to talk to, and way hotter up close.

And here it was; that awkward moment at the end of a first date when you're standing at your door, wondering if it'll be a simple goodnight, a handshake, a hug, or... maybe a kiss?

I felt my nerves creeping up, prickling at my skin.

"I'll see you on Wednesday, then," I said, smiling up at him.

"Could I see you before that?" he asked, catching me by surprise.

Taken aback, I tried not to show too much enthusiasm as he stepped closer, closing the gap between us.

"Would that be alright?" he asked again, as if I hadn't heard him the first time.

Swallowing the nervous lump in my throat, I looked up at him, his eyes soft beneath his dark lashes. "I'm sure... we can arrange something."

His hand lightly touched my elbow, pulling me just a bit closer, and I felt it then—that perfect moment. His other hand tilted my chin up slightly.

"Is it okay if I kiss you goodnight?"

I nodded, feeling breathless. "You can," I replied, licking my lips as they suddenly felt dry.

Then he leaned down, his warm, soft lips meeting mine, and those butterflies began to dance. I leaned in a little more, bringing my hands up to his shoulders. It was light, gentle, and as far as first kisses went, it was pretty perfect.

As he pulled back, that same half-smile on his lips, he chuckled and took a step back down the pathway.

"I'll text you in the morning. Goodnight, Miss Holly." He blew me a playful kiss and gave a small bow before heading back to his bike. I waved, my heart thudding as I hurried inside, feeling it beat loudly in my chest.

It took all my strength to wait until I got into my apartment to squeal with delight.

Chapter Six

When Mrs. Finch called the following morning —much too early—I assumed it was an emergency as I jumped out of bed to grab my phone. But no, she was just letting me know the store would be closed for the day since she and Kieren were going out of town. This was news to me, and it was obviously a last-minute decision.

Assuring me I'd still be paid for the day, she hung up and I fell back asleep, not waking until past eleven. That was unusual for me, but I guessed I needed the extra rest.

I tried not to check my phone too often, hoping Dylan would have messaged by now, but by the time the clock struck one in the afternoon, I was feeling a bit fed up.

With this unexpected free day, I decided to text Jessica, the only friend I had left in town to see if she wanted to hang out. She let me know she wouldn't be home for the rest of the holiday season, so that was a no-go. And to top it off, my parents texted to say they were extending their trip for another week or two and would call me on Christmas morning.

Sighing, I tucked my t-shirt into my jeans, threw on a

sweater and a warm jacket, and headed into town for coffee and some Christmas shopping. I'd already planned to get a nice box of chocolates for the book club ladies and a new pair of gloves for Mrs. Finch—hers were getting a bit shabby.

As I browsed through a display of fridge magnets in a small gift shop, I saw a keychain with a motorcycle on it.

Would it be silly to buy this now? I wanted to help Dylan get into the Christmas spirit, and while I wasn't fully feeling it myself today, this would be a small, light-hearted gift—something simple.

After picking up the keychain, some fluffy socks, and a handmade catnip toy for Usagi, I paid and made my way into the Christmas market.

From across the square, I heard church bells ringing as a small group in formal clothing gathered, watching as a beaming bride and groom burst out of the church into a shower of confetti and dried flower petals.

Their photographer was quick to capture the moment, and I watched from a distance as the crowd cheered, the groom dipping the bride in a heart-stopping kiss. They walked toward the Christmas market, no doubt to snap some winter wonderland photos by the big Christmas tree.

Weddings and marriage were still a little far off in my mind, but I'd be lying if I said the thought hadn't crossed my mind before. My boyfriend in university had once proposed to me on a drunken night, but I'd just laughed, calling him stupid since it happened the day after we broke up.

Now, here I was, back in my hometown with few prospects outside the little bubble I'd made for myself. Sitting down on a park bench with a hot chocolate, I took a moment to watch the scene around me.

For all that I sometimes disliked Jamestown, it wasn't all bad. There was a strong sense of community—everyone looked out for each other, or at least tried to. I spotted Frank across the square, enjoying what looked like a noodle pot someone had kindly given him. I wished I had more space to help him, to get him back on his feet, but countless petitions at town hall and pleas to local B&Bs for him had all been in vain.

Tomorrow, I thought. *I'll ask Mrs. Finch again. Maybe this time we can find a way.*

"Fancy finding you here," Dylan's voice chimed in my ear as he leaned over the back of the bench, startling me.

"Dylan!" I said, smiling as he came around to sit beside me, planting a light kiss on my cheek.

"I thought you'd be holed up with your books," he teased.

"I was supposed to be at work, but my boss and her son are off to the city today."

"Ah, so you're not playing hooky," he winked.

"Do I look like the type who would play hooky?"

Raising an eyebrow, I noticed that my glasses were a little smudged. Dylan must have noticed too because he gently took them off my face and cleaned them with the hem of his dark blue shirt before placing them back on my nose.

"Nah," he said with a grin, "you don't strike me as the type who'd ever dare miss a day of school."

I wasn't sure whether to be offended or laugh because he was right—I hated missing school. Growing up, I'd much rather have been there than at home. My parents were big travellers, always off seeing the world, and having a kid didn't exactly slow them down.

"My granddad was never happy if I missed a day of school, so I didn't. Well, unless you count the time I had my appendix out, or when I fractured my knee rollerblading."

"You lived with your grandfather?" he asked, his brows furrowing a bit.

"My parents were around...sometimes," I replied, looking down. "But they were always off travelling. They're artists—my dad's a photographer for a big company, and my mom would usually go with him. My granddad raised me for the most part." I lowered my gaze as the image of him flashed through my memory, his silver hair, bright blue eyes, and warm smile bringing a pang of grief.

"He died not long after I got back from university. He left me his house, but I couldn't live there, so my parents sold it. I used some of the money to buy my apartment."

"What happened to the rest?"

"College fees, and my parents kept a bit. The rest is in savings now."

Talking to Dylan felt easy—almost too easy—as if sharing my past with him wasn't a big deal. His warm brown eyes stayed on me, absorbing every word. He was wearing the same black jeans as yesterday, but the dark blue shirt was different, and it suited him perfectly.

"Well," he said, "maybe one day you'll feel ready to spend some of it and see the world."

"Maybe... one day," I replied, smiling.

"What brings you into town?" I asked, eager to steer the conversation away from myself.

He fiddled with his keys, and I noticed a car key on the keychain alongside his motorcycle key, as well as several other keys all attached to a patterned lanyard. The design looked familiar, but I couldn't quite place it.

"Grandma's medication," he said. "She had a doctor's appointment and wanted to meet a friend for lunch, so I'm left wandering around until she's ready." He didn't sound thrilled about waiting around; maybe he'd tried to kill time at the bookstore but found it closed, leaving him stuck in a sea of Christmas decor.

"The town really goes all out for the holidays, doesn't it?" he asked, as if reading my thoughts.

"I don't remember it being quite like this when I was a kid. Maybe I blocked it out," I laughed. He leaned forward, resting his forearms on his knees, looking relaxed.

"Why don't you like Christmas?" I ventured, hoping for a fuller answer than the one he'd given me last time.

"That, sweet Holly, is a story for another time."

His phone buzzed, playing a standard ringtone, and as he pulled it from his jacket pocket, I saw "Grandma" pop up on the screen. That was his cue to go, and I wasn't sure how I felt about it. As he stood to leave, he turned on his heel to face me, flashing that dazzling smile with the little dimples again.

"Be ready at seven tonight—I have somewhere I want to take you."

"Is that a request or an order?" I asked, blushing.

"Depends. Which would you prefer?" He leaned down, lifting my chin and kissed me softly before turning and heading across the street toward one of the side streets.

I STOOD on my doorstep that evening, my hands shoved deep into my pockets as I glanced down the road for what must have been the tenth time in the past five minutes. The air was crisp, and I could see my breath forming faint clouds as I exhaled. Pulling my scarf a little closer around my neck, I shifted on my feet, feeling my excitement building.

This was our first real "date." As for the coffee one, well

it didn't really count. And even though Dylan had barely given me any details, something about tonight felt different.

I'd kept it casual—my favourite black turtleneck, a pair of jeans, and boots to keep my toes warm. My hair was left loose, the natural waves falling around my shoulders. Warm but still put together, I thought, glancing at my reflection in the window beside me.

Then I heard it—a low, smooth engine, approaching steadily down my quiet street. Dylan's motorcycle pulled up and he got off, looking effortlessly cool in his dark jeans and a fitted leather biker jacket. Taking off his helmet, he gave me that easy, half-smile as he walked over, hands tucked casually in his pockets.

"Hey, you ready?"

"Definitely," I replied, grinning as he removed a backpack from his shoulders and pulled out not just the helmet, but also a leather biker jacket.

"Put this on." He commanded, handed me the jacket. I eyed him, a little confused as he brushed it off with a laugh.

"You didn't have the proper attire last time, and I want to keep you safe."

"So... are you going to tell me where we're going?" I asked, hoping he might break and give me a clue.

But he just chuckled, shaking his head. "It's a surprise. One I am sure you will enjoy."

As the engine roared to life underneath us, I clung to Dylan's back as we made our way out of town, the familiar streets fading behind us. The road opened up to the countryside, winding along the narrow, tree-lined B-road that led toward the coast.

As we drove further, something caught my eye up ahead —a brilliant array of lights shining against the dark sky. My heart skipped a beat when I realised what it was; a huge funfair, nestled near the beach.

"Are you serious?" I said, glancing over at him, barely containing my excitement.

He gave me a warm smile, his eyes flicking between me and the road. "I thought you'd like it."

I did. The fairgrounds spread out in a maze of twinkling lights and colourful booths, a mix of whirling rides and concession stands. It was nothing like the small fair in town; this one was huge, with a large Ferris wheel that glowed like a giant spinning star against the night sky.

As he pulled into the parking lot, I felt a mix of excitement and nerves. I'd only been here once before, for a school trip, but never with someone like Dylan. I couldn't help but wonder if he felt the same kind of anticipation, the hope that tonight might mean something more than just rides and laughter.

He turned off the bike and looked over at me, his smile soft. "Ready to make some memories?"

I nodded, unable to keep the grin off my face. "Absolutely."

Chapter Seven

As we stepped into the fairground, I was hit by a wave of lights, music, and colour that practically made my heart skip. Everything sparkled and shimmered under the night sky, every ride and booth alive with energy. The smell of popcorn, cotton candy, and fried food drifted on the air, and my eyes widened at the sheer number of rides towering above us, flashing in every colour imaginable.

I turned to Dylan, grinning from ear to ear. "This is amazing!"

He chuckled, watching me with that soft, amused look I was starting to recognise. "So... where to first?"

My eyes locked onto a small roller coaster, its neon tracks looping and dipping, and I didn't hesitate. "The rollercoaster!"

Dylan's expression shifted, and he scratched the back of his neck, glancing at the ride with a slight frown. "Not a fan of rollercoasters," he admitted.

"Not even a little one?" I teased, nudging his arm playfully. "Come on... please?"

He sighed, but the hint of a smile tugged at his lips as he

gave in. "Alright, but only because you look way too cute right now for me to say no."

We made our way to the coaster, and I couldn't help but laugh as he muttered something about how this was definitely *not* his idea of fun. But the moment we strapped in, I was swept away, shrieking with joy as the car whipped around the curves, dipping and turning. By the time we got off, my cheeks hurt from smiling, and I could tell Dylan was trying not to laugh at my excitement, even if he looked a bit pale after the ride.

"Worth it?" I asked, grinning.

He rolled his eyes, but gave me a lopsided smile. "If it made you this happy, then yeah."

The next few hours felt like something out of a dream. We tried everything, from picking ducks in the carnival game stalls to knocking over glass bottles at the shooting gallery. Dylan's aim was shockingly good—he easily took down three bottles and won me a small brown teddy bear with a red bow around its neck. I hugged it to my chest, beaming as he handed it to me.

"For the rollercoaster trauma," he joked and I laughed, feeling a warm flutter in my chest.

We moved on to the cotton candy stand, and Dylan ordered a giant stick of pink cotton candy. I pulled off a piece, tasting the sugary sweetness as it melted on my tongue. We took turns sharing the fluffy treat until our fingers were sticky, and our smiles were even stickier.

Finally, we hit the bumper cars. I climbed in and grinned at him from across the arena as he sat in his car, the lights twinkling around us. The second the buzzer went off, I steered directly toward him, laughing as I bumped into his car with a satisfying thud. He retaliated, grinning as he circled around and aimed straight for me, and we both melted into laughter, chasing each other across the floor until the ride ended.

By the time we climbed out, my cheeks were aching from laughing so much. I looked at Dylan, feeling overwhelmed by how happy I was, how something as simple as a comic book falling on my head had led to this amazing night. This past weekend had changed everything, and it was impossible to ignore how much he'd come to mean to me in such a short time.

As we wandered to a quieter spot under the twinkling fairground lights, Dylan pulled out his phone and turned to me. "Smile," he said, holding the camera up.

I grinned, leaning in close, and he snapped a selfie. I peeked at the screen and laughed at how silly we looked, our cheeks flushed and our eyes bright with joy. Just as he prepared for another shot, he surprised me by kissing my cheek, catching my look of shock as he snapped the picture.

When I looked up at him, he had that playful, teasing smile on his face, but his eyes held something softer, something warm.

"Gotta keep you on your toes," he said, winking.

I rolled my eyes, still feeling the warmth of his kiss on my cheek. As the fair lights sparkled around us, I realised I couldn't wait for whatever came next.

He was keeping me on my toes, and part of me was waiting for the other shoe to drop—for his mood to shift or for me to lose my shine in his eyes, like some new toy that gets tossed aside. I shook my head at my own thoughts and focused on Dylan, watching him walk ahead, his face relaxed as he looked at the sparkling lights.

"Ferris wheel next?" he asked, holding out his hand for me to take.

Linking my fingers with his, I nodded with a smile and we joined the small line of people waiting for a car. Ahead of us stood a group of young adults—two girls laughing with their boyfriends, while two other guys glanced back at us. I noticed them look at us and then exchange glances before one of them called out.

"Hey, Dylan!"

They looked to be about our age, and one of the girls gave me a quick up-and-down look, flashing a fake smile that made me want to shrink back. I wasn't exactly built for handling judgmental strangers—I'd always been too introverted for that.

"Where you been, bro?" one of the guys said, stepping forward and crossing his arms as he looked between me and Dylan. "Thought you'd gone home by now."

Dylan gave me a reassuring side glance, rolling his eyes slightly before answering. "Not yet. Been busy."

"Too busy to hang out with your friends?" the blonde girl said, appearing beside him with a mock pout as she batted her lashes. The whole group had gathered around us now, and I felt a pang of discomfort. They were the type I imagined Dylan would hang out with—trendy, cliquey, and confident. Definitely not like me.

"I found better things to do with my spare time," Dylan said smoothly, ignoring the girl and taking my hand again. The group looked shocked, and I could feel their stares on us.

"Who's your date?" another guy asked, throwing his arm over the blonde's shoulder.

"This is Holly." Dylan's smile softened as he looked down at me, and I felt my shoulders relax. That other shoe still hadn't dropped. "Now, if you don't mind, you're next in line," he said, nodding toward the Ferris wheel operator, who was motioning them to board.

The group huffed, grumbling as they turned to climb the metal stairs and into their car.

"Want to go somewhere else?" Dylan asked me in a low voice.

"If you'd rather, we can," I said, matching his reassuring tone.

He nodded, and we slipped out of line, making our way over to a snack stand where the scent of cheesy fries made my stomach growl. With our fingers still intertwined, he paid for a box to share, and we headed toward the shoreline. The tide had receded, leaving a stretch of cold sand for us to walk along, with the fairground lights in the background, the soft splash of waves nearby, and moonlight illuminating everything around us.

It was beautiful.

Chapter Eight

The salt air mingled with the scent of Dylan's cologne, creating an intoxicating aroma that seemed to swirl around us as we sat close to each other on the cool sand. The night had draped the beach in a velvet shroud, pierced only by the distant twinkle of fairground lights and the moonlight reflecting on the shore. We shared a box of fries, the warmth from the cardboard seeping into my thighs. I plucked one out, twirling it between my fingers before bringing it to my lips, savouring the crispness and the tang of sea-salt.

"Try this one," I said playfully, offering him a particularly long fry with a teasing glimmer in my eye.

Dylan leaned forward, accepting the fry from my hand with his lips, and for a moment our fingers brushed—a jolt of electricity sparking through me. The corner of his mouth curled up in a half-smile as he chewed, his gaze never leaving mine. It was like we were the only two people in the world, wrapped up in each other, the sound of waves crashing against the shore providing a musical backdrop to our secluded intimacy.

"Hey," he whispered, his voice huskier as the ocean

breeze tousled his dark hair, casting shadows across his jawline. In the moonlight, his eyes were deep pools that promised mystery and adventure. My heart raced, thumping a frantic beat against my ribcage.

"Hey," I mirrored back, breath catching slightly. Time seemed to slow, each second stretching out as if it were unwilling to pass and interrupt the moment that hung between us. My skin buzzed wherever it was exposed to the night air, but even more so where it came into contact with Dylan—our shoulders brushing, knees touching.

As the night stretched on towards eleven, the chill of the evening nipped around us, but the heat emanating from Dylan's body was enough to ward off any cold. I couldn't help but lean into him, taking his warmth, feeling his arm automatically wrap around me as it drew me closer into his embrace. Our shared laughter and soft conversation had faded to a comfortable silence, the type that felt full rather than empty, charged with unspoken words and longing looks.

And then, as if the night had slipped away without our permission, Dylan glanced at his watch and sighed, his voice cutting through the bubble of our shared warmth.

"I should take you home."

The words hung in the air, heavy with reluctance, and I knew that neither of us truly wanted the night to end. But reality beckoned. Even so, I wasn't ready to let go—not yet at least.

I turned to face him, the soft glow of the boardwalk lights casting a golden hue on his features. "Maybe," I started, the word hanging between us like a delicate thread of possibility, "we could stay out a bit longer?"

My heart thrummed in my chest, a silent hope that Mrs. Finch would stay on her impromptu holiday, shutting the store for just one more day. It was a risk—I knew I should be responsible, prepare for work in the morning—but the thought of cutting our evening short squeezed my lungs tight with disappointment.

"Or," I continued, the hint of a mischievous smile playing on my lips, "you could come back to my place?" The suggestion sent a current through me, bold and uncharted. Something I wouldn't normally even think to say, this was uncharted territory for me.

Dylan's expression shifted, interest igniting in his eyes as he considered my words. "Let's just get you home first." He winked.

His hand found mine, fingers intertwining as we stood and brushed the sand from our clothes—a silent agreement sealed with a simple touch. We walked back to his motorcycle, the night wrapping around us like a secret. Every step felt charged, each brush of our hands sending sparks skittering across my skin. As Dylan secured the helmet on my head, his fingers grazed my neck, sending a shiver down my spine.

The engine roared to life beneath us, the world becoming a blur of wind and adrenaline as we wound our way through the sleeping streets of Jamestown. Leaning into Dylan's back, I let the vibrations of the bike mix with the rapid beat of my heart.

All I could think about was the invitation I had dangled before us—could I really ask him in? The idea of more kisses not just pecks but something deeper, something that lingered and promised more, consumed my thoughts. In the safety of my apartment, away from prying eyes and the constraints of time, what might unfold between us?

As the buildings passed by in a silent parade, the anticipation built within me, a loudening of desire and decision. Tonight, under a sky dusted with stars, I yearned for the courage to ask for what I wanted—for him to stay, for the night to never end.

The engine's rumble beneath us died, and the world fell into a sudden hush as Dylan turned off his bike. We were just a breath away from my apartment, the pavement cool and shadowed in the evening light. His hands slid under my thighs, lifting me slightly off the bike. A gesture that was both protective and possessive and set me on the ground. The heat of his palms seeped through the fabric of my jeans, imprinting on my hips, igniting tiny fireworks that scattered up my spine.

"Careful," he murmured, voice low and laced with something I couldn't quite name, but desperately wanted to explore.

With shaky fingers, I unfastened my helmet, tugging it off to free my hair, which fell in messy waves around my shoulders. My eyes locked onto Dylan's, and the intensity I found there mirrored the hunger clawing its way through my insides. He leaned in, closing the gap between us and pressed his lips to mine—a swift, passionate kiss that spoke of promises and whispered secrets.

It was nothing like our first kiss—that tentative meeting of lips, the uncertain brush of new desire. This was different; this was a claim. His hands tangled in my strands, pulling me closer, urging me to part my lips. There was a plea woven into his touch, a silent begging that made my heart race and my knees weak.

I yielded, lost in the sensation, in the taste of him—mint and the wild, untamed flavour that was uniquely Dylan. Breathless and dizzy, I allowed the kiss to consume us for what felt like an eternity compressed into a minute or two. My chest heaved against his, our breaths mingling, hot and urgent, until we finally broke apart, gasping for air.

Our foreheads rested together, and for a moment, there

was nothing in the world but Dylan and the thunderous beating of my heart.

The world around us had narrowed to the space that Dylan's presence filled, leaving a charged silence in its wake. He pulled back just enough to search my eyes, his own reflecting the night sky—dark, endless and full of stars not yet seen. The cool wind tugged at our clothes, but the heat that radiated from him was all I felt.

"Are you sure you want to invite me in?" His voice was a low rumble, challenging the steadiness of my resolve.

I caught my lower lip between my teeth, an involuntary reaction as my mind raced with the implications of what inviting him inside meant. The warmth that started in my core was spreading like wildfire, threatening to consume every inch of my being. His question hung between us, heavy with unspoken desires and the knowledge of how easily we could tumble into something irreversible.

My heart hammered against my rib cage, a relentless drum calling me to act on the yearning that had been building since our first encounter. Dylan's gaze never wavered, a silent testament to his patience and understanding. He'd wait for my decision, but the part of me that surged with newfound boldness didn't need a moment more.

I couldn't bring myself to say no—to deny the magnetic pull that drew me to him with such a force. The rational part of my mind flickered, reminding me of caution, of the pace at which hearts should entwine. But as I bit my lip harder, feeling it swell with the pressure, I knew that caution had no place here, not tonight. Not with the way he made the very air around us thrum with possibility.

I had never wanted someone as much as I wanted Dylan right now.

"I want you to come in," the words fell from my lips

before I could second-guess them, my voice a husky whisper betraying the urgency within. Dylan's smile was slow, knowing, and utterly disarming. My heart danced a frenetic samba, pounding out rhythms of anticipation as I reached for his hand. The heat from his skin seared mine with promises as we moved together toward the entrance of my building.

The coolness of the night air gave way to the warmth of the dimly lit hallway, its walls echoing with our uneven breaths as we ascended the two flights of stairs. Each step was a silent drumroll, leading us closer to something neither of us might be ready for, but both of us craved.

At my apartment door, my hands trembled with an intoxicating cocktail of nervousness and desire as they rummaged through the depths of my bag for the elusive keys. Dylan's presence was a solid heat at my back, a comforting yet thrilling pressure that made me feel both protected and wanted. With his hand planted firmly against the door he leaned into me, his lips finding the tender skin of my neck. Each kiss ignited sparks, as he seemed to inhale my coconut-scented hair, along with soothing an ache deep within me.

"Found them," I whispered, more to myself than to him as the key finally slid into the lock, turning with a satisfying click. We stumbled through the doorway, propelled by a hunger that had been simmering between us, now boiling over.

Within moments, we were a tangle of limbs and longing, relearning the geography of each other's lips in a rush. I barely registered the muted meow of Usagi in my consciousness as she darted away, her clairvoyant senses perhaps acknowledging the shift in the atmosphere.

Our clothes became weighty barriers, and with impatient hands, we began to discard them, our movements taking us in a slow, dizzying dance back towards the sanctuary of my bedroom. Our trousers remained a final frontier, yet even through the layers Dylan's excitement was palpable, pressing insistently against me, a testament to the shared electricity that coursed through our veins.

As we collapsed onto the bed, a cascade of sensation overwhelmed me, every touch, every kiss, writing new chapters on our skin, telling tales of passion that neither of us would ever forget.

Dylan's lips traced a path over my skin, each kiss a stroke of admiration that sent shivers cascading down my spine. The flicker of dim light from the bedside table danced across our entwined bodies, casting shadows that seemed to sway with us. His mouth lingered at the hollow of my throat, drawing a gasp from my lips before descending with the same unhurried passion down the valley between my breasts, leaving a trail of warmth in its wake.

"Please," I whispered, my voice barely more than a thread of sound, but he understood it as clearly as if I'd shouted. My fingers tangled in his hair, urging him closer, even as he continued his deliberate descent. The button of my jeans gave way under his deft fingers, and he peeled them off with such ease, it was as though they were no more substantial than mist. With each garment shed, I felt barer, not just in flesh, but soul—stripped for Dylan's eyes to admire without reservation.

I wasn't slender like the women in glossy magazines; my body carried the softness of curves, the tangible evidence of a life lived, of meals savoured, of joy taken in simple pleasures. But in Dylan's gaze, I saw none of the criticism I levelled at myself. There was only hunger there—fierce and unapologetic—and something else that made my heart swell: adoration.

He leaned up then, his eyes never leaving mine as he

pressed a soft kiss to my hip, his breath hot on my skin. That look in his eyes intensified, and I could almost feel the weight of his desire, heavy and electric.

"You're beyond words, Holly." His voice was a low growl that vibrated through me. "You're beautiful."

The words were simple, but they struck deep, resonating somewhere within me that had long been silent. Validation bloomed in my chest, sweet and heady, and I could do nothing but believe him in that moment. The truth was there in the depths of his darkened eyes. It was written in every line of his body, in the rough tenderness of his touch, in the reverence of his kisses.

"Say it again," I breathed, a plea wrapped in a whisper.

Dylan responded by pressing his lips against mine in a searing kiss, his hand cradling the back of my head gently. He pulled away just enough to repeat the words, each syllable etched with intensity, "You're beautiful, Holly. So damn beautiful."

My cheeks burned with a gentle flush, an involuntary response as Dylan's movements shifted. His fingers hooked beneath the hem of his T-shirt, and it was as if time slowed, each muscle flexing and releasing as he lifted the fabric up and over his head. A landscape of sculpted strength revealed itself to me—shoulders broad and inviting, arms that promised both safety and pleasure.

I lay there, awestruck by the sheer masculinity of him, by the curves and planes of muscle that spoke of discipline and raw power. It was a body crafted not from vanity but from purpose, from a life lived fully and embraced with both hands. For a moment, I was lost for words, my gaze drinking in every detail—the ripple of his chest, the tightness of his abdomen, the way his skin seemed to call out for my touch.

The yearning inside me grew fierce, a wave of desire that

wanted to claim him in every conceivable way—to feel those strong arms envelop my curves, to be held tight enough to forget everything else.

But Dylan had other plans. He wasn't ready to grant my silent plea's just yet. Instead, his fingers danced across my skin with a maddening lightness, tracing the edge of my knickers with deliberate slowness. My hips responded without command, arching towards him, silently begging him to end this exquisite torture.

He knew exactly what he was doing; I was sure he could feel the heat radiating from within me, the wetness that was his to discover. And when I moaned—a sound born of frustration and need—it only seemed to stoke the fire in him further.

"Dylan," I found the breath to whisper, my voice tinged with a passion that was new and all-consuming.

With a sly grin that told me he relished my desperation, he obliged, peeling the fabric away and casting it aside like an afterthought. Then he lowered his head, his lips finding the most intimate parts of me.

As his mouth met my flesh, it was as though every nerve ending came alive. The world narrowed down to the sensation of his tongue, exploring and worshipping with dedication. In this moment, Dylan didn't just taste me—he revered me, his actions painting a picture of devotion that transcended the physical realm.

"God, Holly," he murmured against me, the vibration of his voice adding another layer to the symphony of sensations. "You're divine."

And as he continued his tender exploration, I knew that I was experiencing a form of adoration that would forever redefine the essence of my being.

My voice, a high-pitched keening at the edge of pleasure, was all the surrender Dylan needed. He pulled back with a devilish gleam in his eyes and a smirk playing on his lips that could only be described as victorious.

As my chest heaved with short, ragged breaths, I watched him stand at the foot of the bed, shaking off his jeans and then his boxers, I couldn't pry my eyes off him. He picked up his jeans and pulled something from his pocket. He came prepared.

With skilful fingers, he tore open the foil packet he'd retrieved and rolled the condom onto himself—a promise of what was to come. My gaze lingered on him; he was impressive, striking a balance that whispered promises of both pleasure and comfort to my eager body.

"Are you sure?" he asked, hovering over me then, his voice rough with desire yet laced with concern. It was that question—the respect behind it—that lit the fuse of my yearning even more fiercely.

"More than anything," I breathed out, my hands reaching for him, needing to bridge the gap between our bodies.

He aligned himself with my entrance, and as he pushed inside, slowly stretching me, I felt the universe contract around us. It was gentle, but every move was filled with intent, a silent conversation between flesh and soul.

At first, he moved with a restraint that was maddening. But as I adjusted to his size, my body welcoming him deeper, he found a rhythm. And oh, how he felt—each stroke a testament to the control he wielded over his own desire, each thrust bringing me closer to the brink.

I cried out, not once but twice, stars bursting behind my closed eyelids as waves of ecstasy washed over me, leaving me dizzy and boneless in his arms. But he wasn't done yet. With an ease that spoke of strength, he flipped us, placing me atop him like I was the centrepiece of his world.

"Look at you," he whispered, awe colouring his tone as

his hands roamed my body, encouraging me to move. "You're incredible."

Encouraged by his words, I arched back, my hands threading through my hair in a display of abandon while he sat up, his embrace engulfing me. We moved together, a dance as old as time, until finally, his movements grew erratic, heralding the end.

As he climaxed, his eyes never left mine, burning with an intensity that seared itself into my memory. Then, we were collapsing, a tangle of satisfied limbs and shared warmth, sinking into the afterglow of our passion.

Chapter Nine

We'd stayed up talking until the first light of winter sun began breaking through my apartment curtains. Between warm cups of tea and raiding my snack drawer, we eventually fell asleep in each other's arms. Usagi had already decided she liked Dylan, curling up at the foot of the bed, purring contentedly by his feet. When my phone rang, I sent it to voicemail—Mrs. Finch, saying she and Kieren would be out of town for another day but that a delivery was expected around lunchtime, so I'd need to prepare for it at the store.

I didn't want to wake Dylan; he was sleeping so peacefully next to me. I was surprisingly awake though, feeling a strange sense of energy from the past day, almost like I'd been recharged.

For a while, I watched Dylan in the soft morning glow, his features relaxed and warm. As much as I wanted to stay wrapped up with him, I slipped quietly from bed to shower, hoping not to disturb him.

But when I emerged, dressed and dried, I found Dylan's side of the bed empty, his clothes gone. A sense of dread washed over me. Racing to the window, towel still clutched around me, I looked out. His motorcycle was still parked below. My breath hitched, the brief panic flooding me before I heard the front door click open. There he was, looking a bit weary and dishevelled, carrying two coffees and a small bag of donuts.

"Oh, I thought I'd be faster," he said, setting the tray down on the kitchen counter. "I heard you get up and figured we'd need some coffee."

Relief softened the tension in my shoulders as I wrapped the towel around me more tightly. "I...thought you'd left," I admitted, keeping my voice light even though the words held more weight.

"Left?" He looked at me seriously. "I wouldn't do that." His gaze softened, as if sensing the worry behind my words.

Shrugging, I threw on some leggings under my towel and slipped into a t-shirt, carefully avoiding his eyes. "Wouldn't be the first time I've woken up to find someone gone," I mumbled, trying to brush it off.

Dylan stepped closer, lifting my chin to meet his gaze. "Holly, don't ever think that's how I'd treat you." His hand brushed my cheek, and then he leaned in, kissing me gently, tasting coffee and donuts. I felt myself relax, though I hated how much I already wanted him around. The feeling was terrifying.

"Thanks for breakfast," I murmured, wandering over to grab my coffee. Taking a sip of my coffee, I let out an appreciative hum. He'd even remembered my order correctly.

"I do have to get going soon," he said reluctantly. "My grandma will be wondering where I am, and her carers don't come until early afternoon."

"And I have a delivery to prepare for," I replied, meeting his eyes. "Your book might be in it, so you can swing by to pick it up... or, you know, wait until tomorrow as planned."

"I'll have to text you," he said, looking sheepish. "I've got a bit of a guilt trip waiting for me at home." He laughed softly, but it didn't reach his eyes.

I carried the donuts and coffee to the couch and he joined me, sinking into the cushions as Usagi lounged nearby. The morning was still quiet, peaceful.

"I don't expect us to see each other every day," I said lightly, tracing the rim of my coffee cup. "I mean, we both have things to do..."

He shifted, settling in more comfortably. "I wouldn't mind seeing you every day," he admitted, his hand resting on my leg. "Though you'd probably find me grumpy and boring before long."

I laughed softly, though I was startled at how quickly I'd gotten used to these small moments, these simple gestures. "Then you'll have to get used to Christmas, too. Because I am a big lover of it."

He rolled his eyes, but I noticed his expression turn guarded, the light in his face dimming slightly. I felt a shift in the air as he leaned back.

"Holly... please don't push," he said, his tone lower. "I have my reasons. I don't think I'll ever be able to tell anyone why."

Something in his voice made me hesitate, realising how much this weighed on him. He straightened up, his body language tight, and I realised I may have crossed an unseen line.

"I get it," I replied gently, swallowing the questions bubbling up. "I'm here if you ever feel comfortable enough to tell me, though."

He nodded, his face softening as he looked away. The tension hung between us like a weight, unspoken but present. I took a slow sip of my coffee, unsure what to say next.

"Thanks," he mumbled after a moment. "I appreciate it."

THE NEXT FEW days were filled with either seeing each other or texting whenever we got the chance. Mrs. Finch and Kieren returned to the store by Thursday, and it was full steam ahead for the Christmas sale, with both old and new customers coming in. Even the book club stopped by "just to pop in," though they still walked out with two more books each.

Dylan and I spent most evenings wandering through the Christmas markets, heading to the beach, or wrapped in each other's arms, unable to keep our hands off each other. One night, as we lay curled up on the couch watching *White Christmas* on my small television, we shared a bowl of popcorn and at some point, he drifted off beside me, his head resting on my shoulder.

It dawned on me—was this a relationship? Were we more than friends? I hadn't really asked, and from what I'd learned in college, if you had to ask what you were, it usually meant you weren't anything.

With Christmas just over a week away, I wondered about our plans. Although I'd found him something more than a motorcycle keyring, I wasn't sure if I'd be meeting his grandmother, or if I'd be working Christmas Eve since the store was usually packed right up until then.

"Dylan," I whispered, nudging him gently. He mumbled as he stirred.

"Are you staying here tonight?"

He yawned, stretching. "I...should probably go home tonight."

As much as I enjoyed having him here, his grandmother

needed him more. Plus, I missed having my own space after years of living alone.

"Is that okay?" he asked, stretching his shoulders until I heard a small pop.

Watching his muscles flex along his shoulders and arms made me weak at the knees, and if it weren't already so late, I might've pulled him in for round four.

"Of course, silly," I said, smiling. "You look like you could use a night in your own bed."

He kissed me lightly on the cheek before standing up. The last five minutes of the movie played, and I felt a strange pang in my stomach. Maybe I was getting too used to him being here.

"I'll swing by before you go to work in the morning," he said, reaching over to pat Usagi on the head, scratching behind her ears.

"You don't have to. I'm a big girl—I can catch a bus and get myself to work."

He laughed, then knelt in front of me, his hands on my thighs, looking up with those beautiful brown eyes and that dazzling smile.

"I'm not about to let *my girl* catch a bus in this weather." He kissed me softly on the lips, and my heart skipped a beat.

His girl.

Dylan pulled me in for a final warm hug, resting his chin on the top of my head. I let myself sink into his arms for a moment longer, savouring the way his touch wrapped around me, like a blanket of comfort I hadn't realised I'd needed so much.

"Sleep well, Holly." He whispered softly, brushing a final kiss across my forehead before he stepped back toward the door. "I'll see you bright and early."

"Drive safe," I said, offering a smile that felt a little wobbly now that I knew I'd be alone tonight.

He gave me a reassuring wink before heading out, and the soft click of the door closing left the room suddenly quieter than it had been in days.

The silence settled in as I wandered back to the couch, pulling the blanket up to my chin. For the first time in over a week, I was alone. I'd grown so used to the quiet over the years, yet now, it felt different—heavier, as if the room somehow missed his warmth as much as I did.

My thoughts drifted inevitably to Dylan. There was a mystery there, one that grew with each conversation we had. Why did he dislike Christmas so much? He brushed it off whenever I asked, but there was a sadness in his eyes whenever the holiday came up, something buried deep that he hadn't shared. I wanted to reach into that silence, that shadow, and understand what made him distance himself from the season I'd always cherished.

I curled up tighter under the blanket wearing a t-shirt of his, staring absently at the twinkling fairy lights I'd draped over the shelves. If my parents were here, I knew I'd talk to them about it. Mom would have some heartwarming theory, and Dad would be quick to tease, always lightening the mood. The thought made me sigh; they were off on some Austrian mountainside, no doubt having the time of their lives while I navigated all this on my own.

Usagi jumped onto the couch, curling up beside me and I scratched her behind the ears, finding a little comfort in her soft purring. But still, the quiet remained. The past week had been filled with laughter, warmth, and those small, unspoken moments with Dylan. And now, with him gone, I was left with a strange ache, a reminder that I'd already started caring more deeply than I'd expected.

I hugged the blanket around me tighter, wondering if this could be the start of something real. Something worth opening up about.

Chapter Ten

The morning air was brisk, chilling me despite my scarf and gloves as I waited outside my apartment for Dylan. He pulled up a few minutes later on his motorcycle, his usual easy smile lighting up his face as he handed me my helmet.

"Morning," he said, leaning in to kiss my cheek.

"Good morning," I replied, smiling as I slid on the helmet. There was something about the cold morning air and the hum of the motorcycle beneath us that made everything feel wide open, like there were endless possibilities ahead. Dylan revved the engine and we were off, weaving through the quiet streets of Jamestown.

It was a perfect ride until we hit a slow crawl at a busy intersection, stopped by a small accident ahead. I bit my lip, checking the time and feeling that familiar anxiety creep in.

"Looks like we'll be a little late," Dylan muttered, glancing back as if he could sense my worry. "Sorry about this, Holly."

"It's not your fault," I said, patting his shoulder. "We'll get there when we get there."

But by the time we reached the store, I was nearly

twenty minutes late. I hopped off, took off my helmet, and gave Dylan an apologetic smile. "Thanks for the ride."

"No problem," he replied, but as I turned to go inside, he gave me one last look. "I'll be back around closing time."

I nodded, trying to calm my nerves but the moment I stepped inside, my stomach dropped. Kieren was waiting, arms crossed and looking like he'd been stewing in his anger since the second I was due in.

"About time you showed up," he snapped, his voice low but razor-sharp.

"I'm sorry," I began, my voice steady but soft. "There was an accident..."

He cut me off, stepping forward, a sneer curling his lip. "Do you even care about this job, Holly? We give you all this freedom, and you take advantage of it. You think you can just show up whenever you feel like it?"

I took a deep breath, trying to keep my voice level. "Kieren, I told you, there was an accident. I got here as soon as I could."

But he wasn't hearing it. He moved closer, his voice rising. "Excuses, excuses. Just admit it—you're not cut out for this. We keep you on because you're, well... easy on the eyes, but I could find someone better in a heartbeat."

A chill ran through me and I sidestepped him, heading toward the office to take off my coat and bag. He followed, looming over me as he muttered close to my ear, "Maybe if you dressed a little nicer, I'd let the lateness slide."

My breath caught, and a shiver crawled up my spine. Before I could respond, a sudden movement from the doorway made me turn.

Dylan's figure was there, his face a mask of icy fury. In a heartbeat, he crossed the room, grabbing Kieren by the collar and slamming him back against the wall. The room went silent, a charged energy crackling in the air.

"I'd choose your next words very carefully," Dylan growled, his voice deadly low. Kieren's bravado evaporated in an instant, his face draining of colour as he stammered.

"D-Dylan—"

Dylan's grip tightened, his knuckles turning white as he leaned in, his voice barely more than a whisper. "If I ever hear you talk to her like that again, you'll regret it. Do you understand me?"

Kieren swallowed hard, his eyes wide, and I could see the glisten of unshed tears. "Y-yes," he choked out.

"Dylan, please! Put him down!" I begged, my heart pounding as I tried to keep my voice steady. The last thing I wanted was for this to escalate.

Dylan hesitated, his gaze shifting to meet mine. With a final look of contempt, he released Kieren, who stumbled back, slumping against the wall, his face flushed with humiliation.

"I'll see you after my shift, okay?" I murmured, my voice barely above a whisper.

For a second, Dylan looked like he might argue, his jaw clenched, but then he nodded. "Fine." He shot one last glare at Kieren before turning and walking out, leaving a heavy silence in his wake.

The store felt hollow after he left, the air thick with tension. I glanced over at Kieren who had slunk off toward the storeroom, his tail between his legs. I could still feel the slight tremble in my hands as I went back to the counter, taking a deep breath to steady myself.

This job might not be what I wanted forever, but it was what I had right now, and I wasn't about to let Kieren's insecurities or bullying make me lose it. I'd faced bigger problems than him, and I'd get through this too.

By the end of my shift, the store felt empty, Kieren was nowhere to be seen. I didn't mind one bit; it was a relief to spend the last few hours in peace, even if I was still shaken from this morning's confrontation.

Every time I thought of Kieren's words, his snide remarks, it sent a sour pang through my chest. And yet, there was a part of me that felt uneasy about the way Dylan had handled it. Not that I didn't appreciate him standing up for me—I just wasn't sure how I felt about him going so far.

I glanced out the window as I closed up the store, watching snowflakes start to drift down slowly, covering the street in a soft, sparkling blanket. I locked the door and wrapped my scarf tighter around my neck, then scanned the street for Dylan, expecting to see him waiting there.

But he wasn't there.

I checked my phone, thinking maybe he'd messaged me, but there was nothing. I fought back a small wave of disappointment, telling myself it wasn't a big deal. He probably got held up with his grandmother or something—it wasn't like I couldn't get home on my own.

I pulled my hood up against the cold and made my way to the bus stop, brushing off the urge to send him a quick message. As much as I wanted to, I didn't want to seem clingy. I'd catch the next bus and get home on my own.

The wait felt longer in the cold, the gentle fall of snow quickly turning into a thick flurry. Tucking my gloved hands into my coat pockets, I bounced on the balls of my feet, trying to keep warm. Finally, the bus's headlights came into view, cutting through the snowy dusk it pulled up to the stop. Taking a seat near the back, I rested my head against the cold window, wondering where Dylan could perhaps be.

The bus rumbled along, taking me through the winding streets of Jamestown, each one dressed up with twinkling lights and holiday decorations. Normally it would make me smile but tonight, it only reminded me of the way Dylan had looked at me when I brought up

Christmas. That guarded, distant look in his eyes. And then the way he'd practically snapped at Kieren this morning. My stomach twisted with a mix of frustration and worry.

By the time the bus finally pulled up near my apartment, the snow had started falling heavier, coating the sidewalks and street lamps in a thick white dusting. I stepped off, shivering as I adjusted my scarf, and began trudging through the quiet neighbourhood.

The walk gave me a moment to gather my thoughts, but it didn't calm the restless feeling that had settled in my chest.

I wanted to talk to him, to know what was going on in his head. But I couldn't shake the feeling that he was hiding something from me—something about his past.

When I finally reached my building, I was chilled to the bone, snowflakes clinging to my hair and coat. I shook off the cold as best as I could and climbed the stairs to my apartment, my mind still racing. I wondered if Dylan would message me or show up to explain why he'd missed picking me up. But when I unlocked the door and stepped inside, the apartment was quiet, just me and Usagi waiting for him.

With a sigh, I poured some food for her, watching as she trotted over and started eating. I made myself a cup of tea, hoping it would help settle the growing tension in my chest, and curled up on the couch with a blanket, my phone on the table in front of me, silent.

The longer I sat there, the more I felt that familiar ache in my chest, the one that whispered maybe this was too good to be true. The one that told me I should guard my heart, just in case this all fell apart.

I wanted to believe Dylan wasn't like everyone else, that he wouldn't just disappear without a word. But as I sat there, staring at my phone, my hope started to falter.

IT WAS a few days before I saw Dylan again, waiting beside a silver Mercedes parked outside my work. Snow still lined the sidewalks, packed down to a slushy mess, and though the streets were clearer, it was definitely too icy for a motorcycle.

Pulling up my hood, I decided not to stick around to talk. He hadn't bothered with a single call or text, and as far as I was concerned, whatever we had going on was over. I made my way to the bus stop, but he jogged up behind me, calling out my name.

"Holly, wait! Please."

I kept walking but he darted in front of me, blocking my way, his arms out like he wasn't about to let me go without an explanation.

"Please, let me explain."

I hesitated. Part of me wanted to hear him out—maybe there was some valid reason for his silence. But a simple text would have done, wouldn't it? Just some basic respect. Instead, he'd disappeared, and now he wanted to talk?

The streetlamp above us flickered on, casting a dull glow as we stood in silence, his face pleading. My heart beat a little faster; I'd just started to open up to him, and he'd reminded me why I didn't let people in easily. Why I hadn't dated anyone seriously in years.

"It's fine, Dylan—you don't have to explain." I side-stepped him, willing myself to stay strong.

But his hand wrapped around my forearm, gentle but firm. "I want to explain, please."

I let out a sigh, part of me wrestling with itself. Maybe I

was being too harsh. Or maybe I was setting a boundary. Even after messaging him first, he'd just...left me on read.

"You left me on read, Dylan," I said, my voice betraying a crack of emotion. Being ghosted hurt—a reminder of friends, ex-boyfriends, people who'd decided I wasn't worth the courtesy of a reply. I didn't need to go through that again.

He dropped his hand, giving me space but I stayed put, my feet rooted to the ground.

"You can drop me home," I said finally. "But you only get until we reach my front door."

Relief softened his features, and without a word he led me to his car, opening the passenger door. I slid in, immediately grateful for the warmth as the seat's heat pads kicked in. As we drove, he took the long way around, stretching every second of the drive in the silence that hung thick between us. The radio hummed softly with Christmas music, and I was surprised he didn't immediately change the station.

"I wanted to text, to call you," he said, finally breaking the silence. "But I couldn't find the time." His voice wavered slightly, as if he wasn't sure how to explain.

I swallowed down a surge of frustration at his words. *Find the time?* I kept my gaze on the frosted window, not ready to meet his eyes.

"My mom...she showed up out of nowhere." His voice softened, words heavy with exhaustion. "She was in a bad state."

I glanced over finally, seeing the tension in his expression, the weight he'd been carrying alone. There was a shadow there, the raw remnants of what looked like grief. His eyes were rimmed with the telltale redness of someone who'd shed too many tears.

"She needed help," he went on, his voice just above a

whisper. "She...likes to drink. A lot. She was on one of her... come downs. Promising to change, to do better. I had to kick her out though, when I caught her stealing grandma's medication."

Shock rippled through me, but all I could do was reach over and rest my hand on his as he drove. His fingers closed around mine. A tiny movement, but it seemed to help him breathe a little easier.

"She's done this before. I knew she might show up again someday, but this time, it felt...different." He swallowed, his Adam's apple bobbing, his voice barely holding steady. "This time I had to make her leave."

My heart clenched, aching for him. I couldn't imagine what it was like to lose a parent to something like that. My parents weren't around much, but I always knew I could count on them. Dylan hadn't had that, not even close.

"Is your grandma okay?" I asked gently.

"She's alright, thankfully," he said, voice still raw. "I think her memory issues protected her this time. She doesn't remember my mom being there. I'm grateful for that, honestly."

Without thinking, I asked, "Is that why you don't like Christmas?"

He turned onto my street then, his silence stretching as he gripped the wheel a little tighter. For a moment, I thought he might brush me off. But then he spoke, his voice quiet and full of unspoken pain.

"The first time she did this, I was fourteen. Christmas morning. She swore it would be the last time, that she'd be better." He paused, the weight of his words pressing down on me. "But it kept happening. Every Christmas after that was...hard."

The car slowed to a stop outside my apartment, but I didn't want to leave just yet. Not like this. The puzzle pieces were fitting together, and I was finally making sense of the walls he'd built around himself. The reasons why he bristled at the very mention of the holiday.

He turned to me, something vulnerable in his gaze. "Can I come back tonight? We could go for a walk, and I'll tell you everything."

"You don't want to come in now?" I asked softly.

His lips lifted in that familiar half-smile as he brushed a hand along my cheek, gentle but steady. "I would, but there are a few things I need to handle back home. But I'll be back in a few hours. Promise."

I couldn't help the worry in my voice. "How do I know you'll keep that promise?"

He held my gaze, his fingers curling lightly around my chin as he leaned closer. "Holly, I will not leave your side, ever again," he said, the words filled with conviction. He placed a soft, lingering kiss on my lips, his own promise held within it.

"I promise."

Chapter Eleven

The sun had long since set, casting my apartment in the soft glow of the twinkling Christmas lights strung across the windows. They reflected faintly on the snow-dusted streets below, creating a serene and cosy view from my seat on the couch. I held my hot chocolate close, the heat radiating through the ceramic mug, its peppermint aroma filling the room, while Usagi curled up on my lap purring away. On the screen, a classic Christmas film played—the kind where everyone's problems were neatly solved within two hours and snow always fell at just the right moment.

But I wasn't paying attention to it. Not really.

My eyes kept darting to the clock on the wall and then to my phone, lying silent on the coffee table. Dylan had promised he'd come back. And despite the warmth of the room and the sweetness of the hot chocolate, I couldn't stop the restless flutter in my chest.

I told myself I wouldn't get my hopes up, but they were already halfway to the ceiling.

The hours ticked by the movie reached its feel-good conclusion, and still, no knock at the door. A part of me whispered that maybe he wasn't coming after all. But just as I was about to give up and head to bed, a soft knock broke through the quiet.

My heart leaped as I scrambled off the couch, setting my mug on the table and brushing the wrinkles out of my sweater. I hesitated for a second, smoothing my hair and taking a deep breath before opening the door.

There he was, standing under the warm glow of the hallway light. Dylan, looking more ruggedly handsome than he had any right to, with his dark hair slightly mussed and his jacket dusted with snowflakes. He held a big, beautiful bouquet of white and red roses in one hand and, in the other, a tub of cookie dough ice cream.

"I come bearing peace offerings," he said, a sheepish smile playing on his lips.

I blinked, the sight of him rendering me momentarily speechless. He extended the flowers toward me, their sweet, fresh scent filling the doorway. The first time anyone had gifted me flowers, and they were beautiful.

"For you," he added, his voice soft.

"You remembered my favourite ice cream?" I finally managed, accepting the bouquet with one hand while gesturing for him to come inside.

"Of course," he said, stepping in and closing the door behind him. He set the ice cream on the counter and turned back to me, his expression earnest. "Holly, I'm so sorry. For disappearing on you, for not calling or texting. I should've handled things differently. I know I hurt you."

His voice carried a weight of sincerity that made my chest ache. He wasn't just apologising—he meant it.

I placed the roses carefully on the kitchen counter, arranging them in an empty vase I had tucked away. The silence stretched between us as I fussed with the flowers, letting his words sink in.

Finally, I turned to face him, leaning back against the counter. "You really did hurt me, Dylan. I thought...I thought we were starting something good, and then you just vanished. It felt like you didn't care."

He stepped closer, his dark eyes meeting mine. "I do care. More than I know how to put into words. And that's what scared me. I'm not used to this...to someone like you."

"Someone like me?" I asked, my voice catching.

"Someone good," he said simply. "Someone I can depend on—Someone who makes me want to be better. And that terrifies me, Holly."

I felt my heart soften at his words, the raw honesty in them breaking through my lingering hurt. "You don't have to be perfect, Dylan. I'm not looking for that. I just...I need to know I can count on you."

"You can," he said firmly, taking my hands in his. His fingers were cold from the night air, but his grip was warm and steady. "I promise I'll do better. I want to make this work."

I studied his face, the shadows of vulnerability etched into his features. The man who had seemed so sure of himself was showing me the cracks beneath the surface, and somehow, that made me trust him more.

"I believe you," I said softly.

Relief flooded his expression, and he pulled me into his arms, holding me close. His embrace was grounding, the steady rhythm of his heartbeat against mine.

"Now," he said, pulling back just enough to meet my eyes, a small smile tugging at his lips, "how about we eat that ice cream before it melts?"

I reached for the silverware drawer, a chuckle escaping me as the cool metal of the spoons clinked against each other. The simple sound was a reminder that life could still hold such innocent moments despite the chaos.

"Deal. But I get the first bite," I declared, a playful edge to my voice.

Dylan's eyes crinkled at the corners, his earlier hesitation swept away by our newfound truce.

"Only because I owe you," he teased back, the warmth finally reaching those chestnut eyes of his. His smile was like a sunrise after a long night—it spread light, banishing shadows and promising brighter hours ahead.

We nestled side by side on the couch, our knees touching gently as we passed the tub of cookie dough ice cream back and forth. Each spoonful was a shared indulgence, a silent pact that softened the edges of the past few tumultuous days. The Christmas lights, a tapestry of tiny stars, bathed the room in an amber hue, their steady glow like a heartbeat of warmth against the creeping cold outside.

The ice cream, sweet with chunks of cookie dough like buried treasure, seemed to thaw the frost that had lingered between us. With every bite, the weight that had pressed relentlessly on my chest began to lift, its heavy shroud giving way to a buoyant sense of hope that fluttered tentatively in my ribcage.

"Good choice," I murmured, my voice soft but sincere, acknowledging more than just the flavour of our dessert.

"Only the best for you," Dylan replied, his tone light but laden with an undercurrent of earnestness.

And, although words remained unspoken, there was a mutual understanding that we were navigating this new terrain together—awkwardly, perhaps, but genuinely. Our relationship might not have followed the usual script, riddled as it was with starts and stops, with missteps and misunderstandings, but it was uniquely ours.

His arm draped casually around my shoulders, a wordless affirmation of his presence. It was in that simple gesture that I found reassurance; despite the odds, he was here, with me. He'd already woven himself into the fabric of my day-to-day life with an ease that belied the complexity of our connection. After all, he'd called me his girlfriend—a term that felt both thrilling and terrifying, as labels often do when they hold the power to define us.

"Girlfriend," I tested the word quietly, almost to myself, letting it hang in the air, a fragile bubble of reality ready to burst and shower us in its implications.

Dylan looked at me, an eyebrow raised in playful challenge, as if to say, "Yes, and?"

I smiled, leaning into him. Yes, this start was far from smooth—it was raw and real, and as delicately imperfect as the patterns of light dancing across our entwined fingers. But it was enough. It was more than enough.

The credits rolled up the screen, their white letters stark against the black backdrop, signalling the end of our festive escape. Dylan's voice broke through the quiet that followed, a hint of hesitation lacing his words.

"So, what do you wanna do now? Another movie, or should I head home?"

I turned to look at him, really look at him. His eyes searched mine for an answer, but more than that—they sought connection, a silent plea for something neither of us had fully defined yet.

In that suspended moment, something within me shifted. The room felt too big, the couch too spacious. There was too much air between us, and suddenly, I couldn't stand any distance at all. I wanted to close the gap, to erase the uncertainty that cloaked us.

Without a word, I leaned in, closing the inches that seemed like miles, and pressed my lips to his with a enthusiasm that surprised even myself. My hands found his face, fingers threading through the hair at the nape of his neck, pulling him closer, deeper into the kiss.

Dylan's initial shock melted away as he kissed me back just as urgently, his arms wrapping around me, binding us together. His response ignited a fire within me—swift, blazing, undeniable. And in that moment, I knew I wanted all of him—the laughter, the warmth, the late-night ice cream sessions, and the unspoken promises hidden in every glance.

As we finally broke apart, both breathless, there was no need for words. The kiss said it all—it wasn't just a question of staying the night, but a declaration of wanting more, to become tangled in each other's arm's once again.

My breath hitched as I pulled away just enough to gaze into Dylan's eyes, their usual humour now laced with a deeper intensity. The flickering lights from the Christmas tree bathed his face in a soft golden hue, shadow and light playing across his features. My voice, barely above a whisper but clear with resolve, carried the weight of my desire.

"You should stay — I want you to stay."

The corners of his mouth curled into a smile, warm and genuine. He leaned in again, his lips meeting mine in tender pecks that punctuated his words.

"I'm not going anywhere," he murmured against me, each kiss sealing his promise, the growing heat between us rendering the room's chill obsolete.

Usagi, ever the silent observer, lay curled up in her cat bed, nestled among the pillows at the other end of the room. She had long since grown accustomed to our late-night whispers and the soft shuffle of movement. Now, she was a quiet witness to the shift happening between her two humans.

I could feel the urgency rising within us, an electric current that demanded more than kisses and whispered confessions. His body pressed against mine told a story of its own, desires manifesting in ways that left little room for misinterpretation. My hands, emboldened by the surge of adrenaline and want, moved of their own accord. Fingers trembling slightly with anticipation, I made quick work of the button of his jeans that stood as the final barrier to our shared need.

As fabric gave way to skin, I marvelled at the singularity of this moment—each of us eager to explore the landscape of the other's longing.

Dylan's hand encircled my wrist with a gentle firmness, pausing the passion of our actions. His breath was warm against my cheek as he leaned in, his voice low and laced with responsibility. "Holly...protection," he reminded me, the single word carrying the weight of care and consent.

A shock of clarity pierced through the haze of desire, grounding me. I nodded, grateful for his mindfulness in the midst of our passion. With a swift peck on his lips, I disentangled myself from his embrace and bounded off the couch. My heart raced, not just with longing, but also with an admiration for his respect towards our safety.

I dashed to the bathroom, the cold tile a stark contrast to the heated skin of my bare feet. The search was frantic but brief; within moments, I had the foil packet secured in my grasp. The sound of its retrieval echoed slightly against the porcelain surfaces, marking the urgency and importance of this simple act.

Back in the living room, I saw Dylan had shifted, making room for what was to come, his expression a mix of anticipation and patience. I returned to him, condom in hand, my movements fuelled by a mixture of adrenaline and affection. There was no embarrassment, only the mutual understanding that what we were about to share was as much about trust as it was about pleasure.

Climbing atop the sofa once again, I positioned myself over him, ready. A silent affirmation passed between us, and without another word, we began to write the next chapter of our story right there, wrapped in the warmth of the Christmas lights and the promise of the night ahead.

My fingers trembled ever so slightly as I tore open the foil packet, my anticipation making my hands less than steady. Dylan watched my with eyes darkened by desire, his chest rising and falling in a rhythm that matched the pounding in my ears. I caught the corner of my lip between my teeth, focusing on the task at hand.

With deft movements born from a combination of eagerness and care, I rolled the condom down over Dylan, ensuring our safety was paramount to our passion. The moment I touched him, he let out a deep, guttural moan that resonated through the room, mingling with the soft sighs escaping from my own lips. His hand found its way to himself, guiding me, silently pleading for more of my touch.

I couldn't help but smile at his response, feeling a surge of power and affection. My fingers encased him, firm yet gentle, and I began to move. The sight of Dylan losing himself to the sensations I drew sent a thrill through my body. His head tilted back, exposing the vulnerable line of his throat, a testament to the trust he placed in me.

Swept up in the moment, the sounds of our breaths mingling, as I leaned down. I let the warmth of my mouth replace the touch of my hand, enveloping him in wet heat. Dylan's reaction was immediate; a strangled sound escaped him, and his fingers clenched at the fabric of the couch, seeking purchase in a world that had suddenly narrowed down to the connection between them.

I felt a sense of pride swell within me—it wasn't just about the physical act, it was about the closeness, the shared intimacy that pulsed like electricity through every caress. I pumped with both hand and mouth, a synchronised dance of lips and fingers that drove us both towards an edge we were only just beginning to explore.

As Dylan moaned beneath me, the sound was music to my ears, a symphony of pleasure that I conducted with every deliberate movement. This was our crescendo, a harmonious blend of desire and affection, and I revelled in every note.

The symphony of Dylan's pleasure increased into a harmony of moans and praises, his voice hoarse with the intensity of his desire. "Holly," he whispered again and again, each utterance more fervent than the last. His fingers, trembling with need, threaded through my hair, tugging gently, as if guiding me to the rhythm of his own deep yearnings.

I could feel the rising tide within him, the urgency that pulsed beneath my lips and fingertips. But just as he teetered on the brink, his breath hitching, his body tensing in anticipation of release, I pulled away. The room filled with the sound of his disappointed groan, a note of longing that echoed my sudden absence.

With a mischievous glint in my eyes, I rose above him, straddling his hips. The air between us crackled, thick with hunger and expectation. I positioned myself, feeling the heat of him against me, a promise of what was to come. And then, with deliberate slowness, I lowered myself onto him.

Our moans mingled and soared, twin exhalations of fulfilled pleasure. The connection was seamless, natural—as if we were two halves of a whole finally coming together. Every movement was a shared dance, every sensation amplified between us until nothing else existed but the here and now, the perfect union of our bodies and hearts.

Faster and harder we moved, our r passion a tempestuous storm, sweeping away in its wake. Dylan's hands splayed on my hips, guiding me, urging me onward, as he lost himself in me. And as the climax approached, my name on his lips.

With every motion, I felt a powerful sense of control and connection. The way Dylan's body responded to my touch, his moans growing more fervent, fed the flames of my own desire. Every part of me was attuned to him—the hard planes of his abdomen under my palms, the taste of his skin, the sounds he made—a symphony that I orchestrated with each rhythmic movement. My heart raced with wild abandon, each beat a drum echoing our union.

I moved atop Dylan with a blend of grace and urgency that felt as natural as breathing. The wildness in my eyes mirrored the tumultuous storm of passion raging between us. With every thrust, I sought to reach deeper, to claim more of him, as if our very souls were intertwining.

His hands, strong and sure, were splayed on my hips, guiding me, urging me onward. I could feel the heat of his touch through my skin, branding me with a desire that seemed to grow inexhaustibly. I lost myself in the pleasure I gave him, and in return, I drowned in the bliss he offered. Each connection of our bodies was a promise, a silent vow of the high to come.

As I moved faster, harder, the intensity built—a crescendo of need that demanded fulfilment. Dylan's grip tightened, a silent plea etched in every contour of his face. He lost himself in the pleasure just as I did, his eyes reflecting the depth of his passion. In those moments, nothing else existed but the relentless pursuit of satisfaction, the urgent chase toward a shared oblivion.

Our bodies moved together in a wild dance, each movement driven by an insatiable desire that seemed to burn brighter with every passing second. The couch beneath us creaked, its protests drowned out by the symphony of our moans and gasps. It was as if we were musicians playing a piece only we could understand, our rhythms perfectly attune, our climaxes building in tandem.

Heat coursed through my veins like liquid fire, and I could feel Dylan's pulse thundering alongside mine. We moved faster, urgently seeking that peak of ecstasy that beckoned us with the sweet promise of release. The world beyond the confines of this room, of this couch, had ceased to exist. There was only the here and now, only the need that clawed at our very essence.

Then, like a breaking dam, the wave hit us. It crashed over me with such fierceness that my senses whirled. My voice tore from my throat, Dylan's name becoming a sacred chant as I shattered into a million pieces. The intensity of my release set my body shaking, waves of pleasure so acute they bordered on pain.

Dylan's own climax followed close on the heels of mine, his cries mingling with mine in a chorus of completion. He poured himself into me, binding us together in the most primal way.

Exhaustion mingled with euphoria as our breaths gradually found their rhythm again, softness replacing the urgency of moments before. My head rested in the hollow of Dylan's shoulder, my body afloat on the remnants of our passion. The pulsing heat that had driven us now soothed us, and I couldn't help but marvel at the profound union we'd just experienced.

There was something in the way his heart drummed against mine, a steady beat that spoke of more than physical satisfaction. It whispered of shared secrets, of laughter tucked between the lines of everyday conversation, of glances that lingered longer than necessary. This connection—it wove through every gasp and touch, binding us in a tapestry far richer than just carnal desire.

I let out a satisfied sigh, surrendering to the warmth of

his chest beneath me. His arms enveloped me, a protective cocoon from the world outside. The gentle press of his lips atop my head felt like a promise that extended beyond the here and now.

And there, in the quiet aftermath of our storm, the realisation settled within me: this wasn't just about igniting senses or chasing pleasure. It was about finding a harbour in another's soul, riding out life's storms together. In the stillness, wrapped in Dylan's embrace, I understood what it meant to be truly connected—to him, to myself, to this inexplicable thing called love.

Lingering in his arms, I felt the rise and fall of his chest steady into a rhythm that calmed the still-quivering nerves within me. The air around us was heavy with the scent of our mingled essences, a tangible reminder of the unity we'd just celebrated.

"That was amazing," he murmured, his breath warm against my hair, which was now a tousled mane framing my face and spilling over his arm.

I shifted slightly, finding his gaze with mine, reading the echoes of shared pleasure that danced in his eyes. A smile curled the corners of my lips, a silent reflection of the joy blooming in my chest.

"Yes," I breathed out, the word barely more than a whisper, yet it carried the weight of all the emotions swirling inside me. "It was."

In that simple exchange, no grand declarations were needed, for everything profound had already been conveyed through the communion of our bodies and souls.

Chapter Twelve

Morning arrived too soon, sunlight peeking through a slit in the curtains while Dylan slept peacefully beside me. He'd confessed last night to paying the care nurse extra to stay overnight with his grandma just so he could spend more time with me.

At first, I'd felt awful about it—he should have gone home—but he'd waved off my concerns, insisting the nurse was happy for the extra cash, especially with Christmas so close.

Usagi meowed impatiently beside the bed, clearly deciding I'd spent enough time lounging around. There was no such thing as a lie-in with a cat convinced she was perpetually starving.

As much as I hated to leave the warmth of Dylan's arms, I slipped out of bed as quietly as I could. The chill of the wooden floor sent a shock through my feet, and I fought the urge to crawl back under the covers. Sliding into Dylan's oversized T-shirt and my trusty fluffy slippers, I padded into the kitchen to feed Usagi.

The coffee machine hummed to life, the Christmas tree in

the corner still twinkling from the night before. As much as I loved the glow of the decorations, the soft winter sunlight streaming through the curtains brought its own kind of magic.

Curious, I opened the curtains wider and gasped. Jamestown was blanketed in thick, pristine snow, at least seven inches deep. The flakes still fell lazily, and every rooftop, car, and lamppost wore a soft white coat. Dylan's Mercedes sat in the parking lot, barely recognisable under the snow.

"Uh, Dylan?" I called, unsure if he could hear me.

He mumbled incoherently, curling deeper into my pillow.

"Babe, you might want to wake up."

The word slipped out before I could stop it, and butterflies swirled in my stomach. I shook off the feeling and walked back to the bed, brushing the hair from his face. I kissed him softly on the forehead, then on his nose, cheeks, and finally, his lips.

Half-asleep, he pulled me into his arms, his hand tangling in my hair as he kissed me back, slow and deep.

"Now *that's* how you wake a man up," he said, his voice husky with sleep.

I laughed, pulling away. "You should probably check outside."

Rubbing his eyes, he wrapped the blanket around his shoulders and shuffled to the window. A moment later, he pressed his face to the glass, letting out a low whistle.

"Oh, shit. That's...a lot of snow." He turned to grab his phone. "I should call Grandma."

"While you do that, I'll check in with work," I said, already knowing the answer. Mrs. Finch had likely called it a snow day before I'd even woken up.

As expected, her text confirmed it:

"Grandma's fine," Dylan said when he finished his call. He sipped the coffee I'd handed him, then sighed. "The nurse is stuck there too, so she'll stay a while longer. I still hate leaving her."

"She's in good hands," I reassured him. "If anything happens, we'll get to her as quickly as we can."

He nodded, though I could see the tension in his shoulders. Sitting beside him on the edge of the bed, I squeezed his knee.

"So, I guess we're snowed in for the day?" he asked, his lips curving into a reluctant smile.

"Not exactly," I said, grinning as an idea sparked in my mind.

"Holly..." His tone was wary, but there was amusement in his eyes. "What are you planning?"

"You'll need my granddad's old snow jacket and boots."

"For what?"

I jumped to my feet, already excited. "To build a snowman, of course! And maybe a snowball fight, if you think you can keep up."

His laugh was warm, and for a moment, I thought I caught a flicker of Christmas spirit in his eyes.

Chapter Thirteen

I rummaged through the apartment cupboard, the smell of old fabric and mothballs swirling in the air as I finally unearthed my granddad's old snow boots and thick coat. The boots were still in great condition—sturdy, black leather that looked like they could withstand any storm. The coat, however, was a different story. It was an oversized brown parka with a fur-lined hood that had seen better days, but it would do the job.

"Found them!" I called, dragging the coat and boots out of the closet.

Dylan was perched on the edge of the bed, sipping his coffee and scrolling through his phone. When I held up the coat with a triumphant grin, he set his mug down and raised an eyebrow.

"That thing's massive. Was your granddad a giant?"

"No," I laughed, handing it to him. "He just liked his oversized coats. And warmth."

Dylan slipped the boots on first, wiggling his feet into place and stamping them on the floor a few times. "Well, the boots are a perfect fit," he said, standing up. "Let's see about this coat."

He shrugged into it, and I couldn't help but burst out laughing. The coat swallowed him whole, hanging well past his hips, the sleeves too long even when he rolled them up.

"What's so funny?" he asked, looking down at himself.

"It's just...you look like you're wearing a bear." I said, still giggling. "But...you also kind of remind me of my granddad. He always wore that coat when we went sledding or built snowmen. Seeing you in it feels...nice."

Dylan gave me a soft smile, tugging the hood up over his head. "Well, as long as it keeps me warm, I'll take it."

A warmth spread through me that had little to do with the heavy coat or the snug boots. Seeing Dylan enveloped in my grandfather's winter wear—it was like being wrapped in a hug from the past, a reminder that even as life went on, some things, like the love we carry for those we've lost, never truly faded.

Once I was dressed in my warm weather gear, snow boots, thick trousers, a thick sweater and winter coat, we headed downstairs and out into the streets of Jamestown.

The scene before us was like something out of a Christmas postcard. Jamestown's streets had transformed into a bustling snow globe scene, alive with winter's unexpected magic.

Children darted between makeshift igloos, their laughter tinkling like wind chimes caught in a brisk breeze. Snowmen stood at attention along the sidewalks, each adorned with scarves and hats gifted to them by their creators.

Dylan held out his hand, and I gladly took it as we strolled toward Main Street. Although the walk would take a little over twenty minutes, it would be an enjoyable one.

"It looks like we're in one of those Christmas films you love so much." Dylan commented, looping my hand into his arm.

"It's rather magical isn't it? You say Seoul gets snow around this time? Was it like this?"

"Well, the city doesn't close down for a bit of snow, it's still pretty much the same every day. Here, it's different, nicer."

"Calmer I bet?" I asked, looking at the scene around us as we reached main street.

My gaze swept across the street, pausing at the sight of a family huddled close by the town Christmas tree. They cradled steaming cups, noses tinged pink as they sipped hot chocolate that I imagined tasted like liquid comfort.

"Look at them all," I murmured, more to myself than to Dylan. A smile tugged at my lips, heartened by the unity the storm had unwittingly woven. Letting go of Dylan, I was memorised by everyone. Couples traced angels in the snow, their bodies moving in. In the distance, a group of teens orchestrated a snowball skirmish, their battle cries punctuating the air with a soundtrack of mirth.

Dylan turned away from me, his gaze fixed on a toddler bundled up so tightly he waddled like a penguin in pursuit of an elusive snowflake spiralling just beyond his mittened grasp. The sight was hypnotic, the perfect distraction.

I crouched down, hands delving into the powdery snow, fingers closing around a handful and shaping it with swift, practised movements. With a mischievous grin, I took aim. The snowball left my hand with a soft whoosh, arcing through the chilly air to find its target.

"Hey!" Dylan yelped as the icy projectile made contact, snapping him out of his trance as it hit him right on the shoulder. He spun around, a look of mock indignation quickly melting into a wide, open laugh. His eyes sparkled with challenge, the oversized coat making him appear like a playful giant ready for a gentle tussle.

"Those damn kids," I said, jokingly looking around, biting back another laugh.

"Ah yeah, sure, those kids." Dylan scooped up his ammunition, the asymmetrical snowball dwarfed in his large palms. "Game on, Holly."

My eyes widened playfully as a laugh escaped my lips and before I could react, he hurled his snowball in my direction. I squealed and ducked, the snowball grazing my shoulder.

"Is that all you've got?" I teased, scrambling to make another snowball.

What followed was a full-on snowball fight, laughter echoing through the streets as we darted between parked cars and ducked behind trees for cover. Dylan was surprisingly quick, and more than once, I found myself hit squarely in the back or arm. But I had my victories too, landing a perfectly aimed shot to his face that made him sputter and laugh all at once.

As we caught our breath, standing in the middle of the snow-dusted street, I couldn't stop smiling. My cheeks ached from grinning, and my gloves were soaked through, but I didn't care.

"You're sneaky, you know that?" Dylan said, brushing snow off his face as he walked toward me.

"Just keeping you on your toes," I replied with a smirk.

"Remind me never to turn my back on you in a snowstorm," Dylan said, brushing snow off his face as he walked toward me, his eyes crinkling with amusement.

"Oh, I'm full of surprises," I replied with a smirk, reaching up to brush snow from his collar.

For a moment we stood there, surrounded by laughter and the faint jingling of sleigh bells from someone's speaker. The world around us blurred, the cold biting at my cheeks forgotten as Dylan reached out, brushing a stray snowflake from my hair.

"You're something else, Holly," he murmured, his voice low and warm. "I think fate dropped that comic on your head just for me."

My cheeks burned—not from the cold this time—as his words sank in. "I wanted to say hi the moment you walked in that first time," I admitted, lifting my eyes to meet his, just a breath away from him.

His hand grazed my face, brushing a strand of hair behind my ear. Then, he leaned in, and his lips met mine. It wasn't just a kiss—it was warmth and snowflakes, everything that made my heart sing and my head spin. I never wanted it to end.

"Shall we grab a hot drink and warm up?" Dylan asked, pulling his lips from mine, his forehead resting gently against mine.

I nodded. A hot drink sounded perfect right now. The café came to mind—its owner lived upstairs, and I was pretty sure the waitress lived just a street or two over. As we stepped inside, warm air from the heaters wrapped around us like a blanket, melting the chill from our skin.

"Be right with you! Grab any seat," called the waitress, balancing a tray as she served another table.

Dylan's fingers stayed threaded through mine as we moved through the crowded room. Clearly, we weren't the only ones seeking warmth; most of the tables were full. Thankfully, we found a small table tucked away at the back.

"How far is your grandma's from here?" I asked once we'd settled in. Now that I thought about it, I realised I didn't even know where Dylan lived.

"It's about a fifteen-minute walk," he replied. "Faster if I drive, but..." He trailed off with a shrug.

When the waitress came over, we ordered hot chocolates

and decided to share a slice of apple pie. As I wrapped my hands around the warm mug, the heat seeped into my fingers, easing their stiffness.

"We could walk it," I suggested tentatively. "Or I could ask around to see if someone with a truck could drop you off?"

I didn't want to impose on Dylan, knowing how much he must be worried about his grandmother. Even if he didn't show it outright, I could see it in his eyes, the way his smile faltered slightly when the conversation veered toward her.

"We could walk," he said, hesitating as he studied me. "But won't you be too cold?"

Truthfully I was freezing, even with my coat and scarf, but if walking was what he wanted, I'd tough it out. His happiness mattered more than a little discomfort.

Watching him drop a spoonful of sugar into his hot chocolate, I couldn't help but admire him. Dylan was effortlessly handsome, the kind of man I never imagined would look twice at someone like me. And yet, he did. He saw me, even when I struggled to believe it myself.

"Give me your glasses," he said suddenly, holding out his hand. "They're smudged from the snow."

I blinked in surprise, then slipped them off, handing them over. He cleaned the lenses with the hem of his t-shirt, the simple gesture making my chest tighten in a way I couldn't explain. When he slipped them back on my face, everything came into focus again.

"They were awful," I admitted with a small laugh.

"I figured," he teased, tapping my nose playfully before taking another sip of his drink.

"If you want to meet my grandmother, we could walk," he offered, his tone softening. "But I think it's better to wait. She'll be a little off because I wasn't there last night. Maybe this weekend?"

I smiled, even though a flicker of disappointment tugged at me. He was right, of course. His grandmother's health came first, and it made sense to wait.

"That sounds like a good plan," I said, keeping my voice light.

He nodded, setting down his mug. "I should check in with the nurse and see how things are going. Maybe I'll walk, or I'll see if someone can give me a ride."

Dylan stood and slipped outside to make the call, leaving me at the table with my half-finished hot chocolate. The warmth of the café suddenly felt less comforting without him there, the chatter of the crowd dulling into background noise.

As I watched the snowflakes swirl outside the window, I couldn't help but hope that, despite everything, Dylan would let me be a part of his life—and his grandmother's—in a bigger way. Soon.

Checking my phone, I wasn't surprised to find no notifications. Jess—though I'd still call her a friend—had been distant for nearly a year now. That friendship had clearly run its course. As for my parents, I knew not to expect anything until Friday, when they'd either confirm their plans to come back for Christmas or announce yet another last-minute change. Mom was unpredictable like that.

The sound of Dylan's boots on the floorboards pulled me from my thoughts, and I glanced up as he returned. He sat down next to me, his shoulders dusted with snowflakes and wasted no time in stealing my warmth. With a tug around my waist, he pulled me closer, his arm wrapping snugly around me.

"Grandma's fine," he said, his voice low but reassuring. "She's alert, and the nurse said her boss suggested she stay overnight just in case. But I think it's best if I head home. The snow's not as bad now—the roads are starting to get cleared up." He paused to take a sip of his drink, licking his lips before adding, "I'll walk you back first, and then try the drive if that's okay with you."

"You don't need my permission, silly," I teased, nudging him with my shoulder. "Just as long as you drive safely and don't go doing donuts or something."

Dylan chuckled, the sound deep and warm before leaning over to press a light kiss to my cheek. A shiver ran down my spine, and I bit back a smile as the butterflies in my stomach fluttered into overdrive.

"Well," he said, his tone dropping playfully, "whenever you're ready, we'll head back. But I won't leave right away—there's something else I'd like to do with you first."

The wink he gave me was paired with that teasing, dimpled smile I was quickly growing addicted to.

"Oh?" I asked, raising an eyebrow but already guessing where this was going.

"It's a good way to warm up," he murmured, leaning in slightly as his voice dipped lower.

I tried to keep my cool, but the blush creeping up my cheeks gave me away. "You're impossible," I mumbled, my words fluttering out as I looked away, only to feel his eyes on me, amused and utterly irresistible.

Chapter Fourteen

The sleet came down in a relentless drizzle, drenching the world in a dreary grey that seeped through my bones. I sighed with relief when Dylan pulled up in his car—a rare concession to the weather over his beloved motorcycle. The door swung open and I hopped inside, grateful for the escape from the icy air nipping at my cheeks.

"Ready for an adventure?" he asked, his eyes crinkling with a smile as he turned up the heat.

"Depends on where you're taking me," I teased, tucking my hands under my thighs for warmth.

"Grandma's been asking about you." he said, and I could tell by the sincerity in his voice.

"Really?" My heart fluttered with a mix of surprise and nerves. "I should probably change out of this," I said, gesturing to my work uniform, which still bore the faint stains of the coffee Kieren had *accidentally* spilled on me that morning. I decided not to tell Dylan—he'd probably march back to the store and pick another fight with Kieren.

"Let's swing by your place first. Need to make sure you're comfortable."

Minutes later, we were back at my apartment, and I was rummaging through my wardrobe for something more presentable to wear to meet Dylan's grandmother. After much deliberation, I settled on a dark purple turtleneck sweater—cosy yet tidy—and paired it with black skinny jeans and my trusty Vans. Adding my thickest coat to fend off the persistent chill, I turned to Dylan, a twinge of nervousness creeping in.

"Look okay?" I asked, putting my hair into a loose plait.

He gave me a long, appreciative look before nodding. "More than okay."

His gaze warmed me as much as the snug outfit, and I couldn't help but smile as we stepped back into the wintry world outside.

We left the sanctuary of my apartment, bracing ourselves against the wintry mix. As Dylan drove, the familiar streets gave way to roads less travelled, and my curiosity piqued. What kind of woman was Dylan's grandmother? Would she approve of me?

"Your grandma... what's she like?" I ventured, watching the wipers battle the sleet.

"Strong. Kind. Rather funny, but you'll see for yourself." He said, focusing on the road.

I nodded, silently rehearsing greeting lines in my head, each one echoing with the weight of first impressions. With Dylan beside me though, I felt an ember of courage flickering to life. And despite the frosty weather and the churn of nervous energy within me, I couldn't help but feel warmed by the thought.

We were getting closer it seemed as we turned into a lane lined with tall, stoic pine trees that stood like guardians, their branches dusted with the remnants of snow. It was the kind of scene I'd only ever encountered in the pages of well-worn romance novels.

"Just up here," Dylan said, his voice pulling me back from my thoughts.

When the house came into view, I caught my breath. The large, detached home exuded warmth, its dark blue front door standing out like a beacon against the snowy landscape. Twinkling lights adorned the porch, casting a soft glow over the small Christmas tree nestled in the corner.

"It's beautiful here," I murmured, almost to myself.

Dylan heard me and smiled, his hand finding mine for a reassuring squeeze. "Yeah, it really is."

As we approached the house, the crunch of snow underfoot mingled with the distant chirping of birds. The festive decorations surprised me; they seemed at odds with the man who shrugged off Christmas traditions so easily.

"I thought you didn't like Christmas," I said, letting a playful edge creep into my voice.

Dylan paused, his hand still clasping mine, and turned to meet my gaze. His eyes softened, a rare tenderness surfacing. "Grandma loves this time of year," he said simply. "Whatever makes her happy."

Something in the way he said *happy* tugged at my heart. I could see it clearly now—the love that drove him to set aside his own feelings for someone he cherished.

As we climbed the steps to that inviting blue door, the Christmas tree lights twinkled in his eyes, and I realised there was so much more to Dylan than the cool, guarded man I'd first met. Maybe there was a part of him that enjoyed the glow and glimmer of the holiday season after all.

The door swung open before we even had a chance to knock, and a wave of warmth and cinnamon wrapped around us like a comforting embrace. Dylan's grandmother stood there, her silver hair framing her face in a neat bob, her eyes twinkling as brightly as the Christmas decorations around her.

"Come in, come in!" she exclaimed, ushering us inside with a graceful sweep of her hand. Her gaze landed on me, and she smiled warmly. "I'm so glad you could make it, dear."

My cheeks flushed at her kind words, and any nervousness I'd felt melted away under her genuine welcome. She led us into the living room where a fire crackled merrily in the fireplace, its golden glow dancing across the room.

"It's lovely to finally meet you, Holly! I've heard so much about you."

I glanced at Dylan as he hung up our jackets. His expression was somewhere between embarrassed and amused, but he said nothing. Slipping off our shoes, we replaced them with slippers neatly waiting in the hallway—something that must have been a long-standing custom in this house.

Dylan's grandmother was a force. Though petite compared to Dylan's towering height, she carried a commanding presence, her warmth filling the room effortlessly.

We settled into plush armchairs by the fire as she bustled off to the kitchen. Dylan leaned closer and whispered conspiratorially, "You're going to love her baking."

His enthusiasm made me laugh softly. Seeing this playful side of him, eager and almost childlike, was endearing.

When his grandmother returned, she carried plates of freshly baked cookies and steaming cups of tea. My taste buds instantly delighted in the buttery, crumbly cookies, and the tea warmed me from the inside out. As we chatted, she shared stories of her youth, punctuated by Dylan's groans and protests whenever she veered into tales from his childhood.

"I missed so much of Dylan growing up," she said, reaching out to cup his cheek fondly. "But now, my boy is back where he belongs."

Dylan smiled at her, a mouthful of cookies muffling his response. "I love you too, Grandma."

The cosiness of the house, the soft crackle of the fire, and the laughter-filled conversations made the hours slip by. As the sun began to set, Dylan excused himself to prepare her evening medication. I followed him into the kitchen, leaning against the counter as he methodically popped pills into a small cup.

"She seems in such good spirits," I said.

Dylan nodded but didn't look up. "It comes and goes. She'll start to fade a little now—it's always harder in the evenings."

His voice was steady, but the weight behind it wasn't lost on me. I watched him carefully measure her medications, and my heart ached for him. This wasn't just caregiving—it was love in its rawest, purest form.

When we returned to the living room, she was leaning back in her chair, eyes closed, her face peaceful. The nurse arrived soon after, and Dylan quietly briefed her on the day's events while I lingered by his grandmother, watching her rest.

As we bundled back into our coats and stepped outside, the snow began to fall again, soft and quiet against the night.

"Would it be alright if I don't come in tonight?" Dylan asked as we reached my apartment.

"That's fine," I said with a smile. "She's lovely, by the way."

"I told you that you'd like her." His voice softened. "I'm glad she was having a good day—and that she'll be able to remember meeting you."

Happiness warmed my chest at the thought of being welcomed into his family, even for just a day.

"Grandma mentioned that you should come to ours for Christmas dinner," he added as he parked the car. "That is, if you don't already have plans."

My smile widened. "That sounds wonderful. I don't have plans, so yes, I'd love to."

The thought of spending Christmas with Dylan and his grandmother filled me with excitement. It was a far cry from the lonely evening I'd imagined, just me, Usagi, and a microwave meal.

"Awesome! I'll come by on Christmas morning to pick you up, and we can head over for lunch."

"Perfect," I replied.

Before I could step out of the car, Dylan leaned over and kissed me softly. It was a kiss that said more than words could—gratitude, affection, and something deeper I wasn't ready to name.

"I'll see you on Christmas morning," I said, my voice barely above a whisper.

"You'll see me before that," he teased, a grin tugging at his lips. "Christmas is too far away."

"It's in two days," I pointed out with a laugh.

"Exactly. Too long to be away from you."

Rolling my eyes, I giggled as he kissed me again, his hand slipping around the back of my neck to pull me closer.

Chapter Fifteen

The first rays of morning light streamed through the small gap in my curtains, waking me from my deep sleep. At first I simply laid there, cocooned in my flannel pyjamas and tangled blankets, listening to the faint hum of the radiator and Usagi's gentle purring at my feet.

It was Christmas morning.

Rolling over, I grabbed my phone from the nightstand and checked the time—just after eight. Dylan wouldn't arrive until late morning, so I had a few hours to myself. It wasn't a bad thing; I'd been looking forward to this quiet time, just me and Usagi.

Well, and the fact I needed to prepare for Christmas dinner with him and his grandma. I'd wrapped his motor-cycle keyring up, got him a pair of fluffy warm socks, the third book in the series he'd been reading and for his grandma, a lovely box of chocolates and a warm knitted scarf. The presents wrapped in red wrapping with silver bows sat on my kitchen counter, patiently waiting.

Sliding out of bed, I tugged on my thick knitted socks, the ones with little snowflakes on them, and shuffled into the kitchen. Usagi followed close at my heels, weaving figure eights around my ankles and letting out her morning demands.

"All right, all right," I muttered, opening her food cabinet. "Merry Christmas to you too."

Once she was happily munching away, I filled the kettle and set it to boil, the familiar whistle echoing through the cosy space a few minutes later. I made myself a cup of steaming Earl Grey tea, adding just a touch of honey before heading to the living room.

My apartment was bathed in a warm glow from the string of fairy lights wrapped around the Christmas tree, their soft twinkle dancing off the baubles I'd carefully hung. The tree wasn't massive, just big enough to make the space feel festive, topped with a star that tilted slightly to the left.

Curling up on the sofa, I pulled my favourite plaid blanket over my legs and set my tea on the side table. Usagi leapt up and made herself at home on my lap, her tiny body a welcome source of warmth as she nestled in.

The classic Christmas movies were already playing on the TV, but I was mostly excited for the Christmas parade. I loved all the vibrant floats as they made their way down snow-dusted streets, accompanied by cheerful commentary and an upbeat soundtrack of holiday classics. I sipped my tea slowly, letting its warmth seep through me as I watched a film of Santa Claus saving Christmas.

For a while, I allowed myself to simply *be*. No rushing, no worrying about the day ahead—just enjoying the stillness of the moment. The world outside felt hushed, wrapped in a blanket of frost and snow, but here, in my little sanctuary, it was cosy and bright.

I thought about Dylan. About the smile he'd given me when he promised he'd come over today, his excitement at sharing Christmas dinner with me and his grandmother. A soft smile crept onto my lips as I imagined him teasing me about something ridiculous, just to see me blush.

But there was a pang of loneliness too, one I hadn't quite shaken. This was my first Christmas without my parents in town, and while I'd grown used to their absences over the years, today felt...different. The holidays were meant to be about family, and though I was grateful for Dylan, I couldn't help missing my own.

Eventually, I glanced at the clock—it was almost ten. Dylan would be here soon, and I should probably start getting ready. But for now, I stayed right where I was, snuggled under my blanket with Usagi on my lap, the glow of the tree and the hum of the TV wrapping me in the simple, quiet joy of Christmas morning.

I was just beginning to pour myself another cup of tea when the doorbell went, and a smile crossed my lips. Dylan was a little earlier than expected and I was half dressed.

"Coming!" I called out, tucking a stray lock of hair behind my ear. My heartbeat kicked up a notch as I approached the door; Dylan's arrival was always like the beginning of a different kind of Christmas magic.

I opened the door to find Dylan standing there, his signature mischievous smile in place. He didn't say a word before stepping forward, winding his arms around my waist and pulling me close. Then, without hesitation, his lips met mine in a kiss that stole my breath. It was deep and deliberate, a kiss that said more than words could.

When he pulled back, his forehead rested lightly against mine. "Merry Christmas," he said, his voice low and warm.

"Merry Christmas to you too," I replied, my cheeks flushed.

"Sorry for the dramatic entrance," he chuckled, brushing his thumb over my jawline. "But I thought it might make the morning a bit more memorable."

I laughed, shaking my head as I stepped aside to let him in. "It's certainly a start."

After making us both cups of tea, we settled on the sofa. Usagi claimed his lap almost immediately, much to his amusement, as I placed his gifts alongside a beautifully wrapped Christmas gift bag he'd brought.

"Ladies first," he said, handing me the bag.

Inside, I found three neatly wrapped packages in silver snowflake paper, each tied with a ribbon. The calligraphy on the tags caught my eye immediately.

"Your handwriting is beautiful," I said, admiring the elegant script.

"Just one of my many talents," he joked, motioning for me to open the first package.

Carefully unwrapping the medium-sized gift, I uncovered a maroon velvet box. My breath caught as I lifted the lid to reveal a delicate silver necklace with a sparkling snowflake pendant.

"Dylan, it's beautiful," I whispered, holding it up to the light. The pendant shimmered as if it held its own tiny bit of Christmas magic.

"Here," he said, taking the necklace from me and gesturing for me to turn around. I lifted my hair, and he clasped it around my neck. When I turned back to face him, his smile was soft, almost shy.

"It's perfect," I said, my voice thick with emotion.

"Open the next one," he urged, his excitement contagious.

The smaller package contained matching snowflake earrings, which I promised to put on once I finished getting ready. Finally, the largest box revealed a motorcycle helmet.

"I thought I already had one?" I asked, raising an eyebrow.

"That was just a spare. This one is yours," he said,

holding it up to show me. My eyes widened as I noticed the faint snowflake pattern decorating the back of the helmet.

"The snowflakes..." I began, my voice trailing off.

He set the helmet down and took my hands in his. "I used to hate the snow. It reminded me of things I'd rather forget—Christmases back in Seoul, my parents, all of it. But then, after spending that day in the snow with you, all those bad memories started to fade. You gave me something better to hold on to."

Tears pricked my eyes as his words sank in, a warmth blooming in my chest. I pulled him into a tight embrace, burying my face against his shoulder. "You softy," I mumbled, laughing as he chuckled against me.

"Now open yours," I said, pulling back slightly to gesture toward the gifts I'd prepared for him.

"They can wait, I have one more thing I want to give you." he said, brushing a stray strand of hair from my face and lifting up my chin to look deeply into my eyes, his hunger clearly dancing there.

"And what's that?"

"The best Christmas orgasm you could ever get."

A laugh erupted from my own chest as he brushed his lips against mine. He was smooth, and I melted like butter. Christmas presents most certainty could wait while he had his way with me. He leaned in then, kissing me in a slow and all-consuming kiss. His hand cupped the back of my neck, drawing me closer until the world seemed to fall away, leaving just the two of us.

He pressed me against the sofa, deepening our kiss, my back resting against it as his tongue danced with mine. Wrapping my arms around his neck, pulling him closer, I could already feel his arousal beating against his trousers, desperately trying to break free. His hands roamed over my body, sending shivers down my spine. I moaned softly against his lips, feeling desire building up inside me.

He broke the kiss and gazed down at me with dark eyes full of hunger. "I want you," he whispered, his voice hoarse with need.

"You already have me."

Without another word, he lifted me up in his arms and carried me across the room to my bed. The warmth of his body against mine sent sparks flying through every nerve in my body. He laid me down gently on the bed before shedding his own clothes.

My eyes roamed hungrily over his naked form as he crawled on top of me. He kissed a trail from my lips to my neck, nibbling and sucking on my skin until I was writhing beneath him.

"Please," I begged, unable to bear the ache between my legs any longer.

He didn't need any more encouragement. Lifting my t-shift over my head, he began to trail kisses down my body until he reached my panties. With one swift motion they were gone, and he buried his face between my thighs.

The pleasure was overwhelming as he flicked and teased me with his tongue. My hands fisted in the sheets as I moaned uncontrollably. It wasn't long before I reached my climax with a cry of pleasure.

As I came down from my high, he moved back up to kiss me again. This time, I could taste myself on his lips and it only turned me on more.

Shifting off me for just a second, he put on a condom and then he positioned himself between my legs as he slowly entered me, filling me up completely. I wrapped my legs around him, pulling him closer as he started to move in a steady rhythm. Every thrust sent waves of pleasure through my body, making me moan and writhe beneath him.

Our bodies moved together in perfect harmony, and I could feel the heat building up inside me again. His hands roamed over my body, teasing and caressing every inch of skin they touched. Lifting me up to sit on his lap, I moved up and down slowly, the tension between us building as we looked at each other with looks of deep affection and lust.

His hands ran up my spine, his fingers finding my hair, tangling in them and tugging lightly to pull my head back and expose my neck so he could place delicate kisses all along the soft skin there.

The pleasure was intense, and I could feel my body trembling with each thrust. His lips found mine again, kissing me hungrily as our bodies moved together. My hands roamed over his broad shoulders, feeling the muscles flex beneath my touch.

He shifted slightly, lifting me off his lap and laying me back down on the bed. He pulled out of me for just a moment to tease me as his fingers replaced his cock. I could feel myself begin to climb that mountain of pleasure again desperately calling out his name as I reached my peak, breathless and wanting more.

As my body trembled with pleasure, he continued to move his fingers expertly inside of me. His lips left mine and trailed down my neck, leaving a trail of fiery kisses in his wake. My hands gripped the sheets tightly as I felt myself getting closer and closer to another climax.

"Dylan," his name was said in a needy, begging tone, incapable of forming any other coherent words as the pleasure consumed me.

With a smirk, he removed his fingers and positioned himself back between my legs. He entered me once again, filling me up completely as he started to move at a slow and steady pace.

The sensations were overwhelming as we moved together in perfect sync. Every touch, every kiss, every thrust was pure bliss. Our bodies were slick with sweat, and our moans filled the room as we lost ourselves in each other.

The sensation was even more intense this time. I wrapped my legs around him, pulling him closer as he started to move in a steady rhythm. Every thrust sent waves of pleasure through my body, making me moan and writhe beneath him. Our bodies moved in perfect sync with one another, and I could feel the heat building up inside me again.

His hands roamed over my body, teasing and caressing every inch of skin they touched. Our eyes locked as we moved together, our breaths coming in short gasps. The desire was building up inside me until it reached the very highest of highs, and I cried out his name loudly as I came undone beneath him.

He followed soon after, groaning my name as he reached his own climax and we collapsed onto the bed in a tangled mess of limbs and sweaty bodies.

For a few moments we lay there catching our breaths before he pulled out of me gently and disposed of the condom. He lay back down next to me, pulling me close so that our bodies were pressed together once again.

"I never want to leave this bed," he said with a lazy smile on his face.

I laughed softly, snuggling closer to him. "Me neither."

"That was amazing," I whispered against his chest.

"Merry Christmas," he replied with a satisfied smile.

We lay there for a while longer, basking in the afterglow of our lovemaking. Eventually, we got up to shower together, enjoying more of each other's company and bodies. How I was walking after it, I wasn't too sure.

Settling down on the sofa, I demanded he open the rest of his presents. I couldn't help but feel overwhelmed with happiness. This was truly one of the best Christmases I had ever had.

After all the presents were opened and the mess was cleaned up, we watched a cheesy holiday movie on TV. He turned to me with a serious expression on his face.

"I have something very important to tell you Holly," he said, taking both my hands in his.

"And that is?"

"Well, two things actually. First one is—are you okay with being mine now? And secondly, I could really go for some turkey right about now."

I wasn't sure if I should laugh, cry or just fall into his arms. I ended up doing all three, crying from laughter as I kissed him again and again.

"You're a dummy. Of course, I am yours. You had me from the moment the bell rang in the store. And as for dinner, yes please I'm starving!"

We were both smiling as we got dressed and wrapped up, ready to venture back outside into the cold. Dylan and I headed towards his grandma's, and possibly towards the rest of our lives together as the snow fell around us.

The End

Acknowledgments

As this book is short and sweet, I'll try to keep these acknowledgments just as brief.

This novella was a bit of a last-minute adventure. Somewhere between writing my next book (set to release in January 2025) and preparing for the holidays, I decided I *needed* another Christmas-themed story. Clearly, I thrive on chaos and love a good deadline!

There are so many amazing people who helped bring this book to life, and I couldn't have done it without you.

First, to my incredible beta team: Karissa, Sydney, Zoe, Kylie, Stephanie, Jeanette, and Gemma. You girls are an absolute dream, and I'm beyond grateful for your support and feedback—especially with my whirlwind timelines!

To my editor, Nikki: Thank you for stepping in at the last minute and turning this book into something truly special. Your input was exactly what I needed.

To my husband, Jack: Your unwavering support for every wild story idea I dream up means the world to me. You are, and always will be, my rock.

To the amazing British Author girl squad! You remind me daily that I'm never alone in this crazy writer's journey. Thank you for your friendship, encouragement, and endless laughter—you're truly a godsend.

And finally, to *you*, my readers: I count my blessings every day for each and every one of you. Your support allows me to follow my passion, and I couldn't be more grateful.

Wishing you all a Merry Christmas and Happy Holidays!
See you in 2025 for more adventures!
With love,
Mel xx

About the Author

Melanie Davies began writing when she was in her early teens, starting off first in vampire role play forums, she began to learn her voice and teach herself how to write creatively. Writing has always been a dream of hers and one she is excited to achieve.

Also By

A DANCE OF TWILIGHT

A fae filled magical world, following the story of Ornella and her Shadow Man. This is the first book in this World Series.

Each book will follow a different couple and can be read on own.

A Dance Of Twilight

MEET ME ON THE ICE - STANDALONE

A stand alone contemporary holiday romance.

Meet Me On The Ice

THE MIDNIGHT STAKES SERIES

A paranormal romance inspired by Van Helsing and Buffy the vampire slayer. Filled with found family, spice, a badass female lead and a mysterious male lead.

Graveyard Shift - Taken To The Grave

NIMRA WORLD SERIES

A fantasy romance full of unforgettable twists & turns, found family, a strong

female lead, and a morally grey mc. Slow burn to spice, multi-pod.

The Sapphire Oath | The Emerald Truth